A Hole in Her Sky

Erik Daniel
Shein

Melissa
Davis

Karen
Fuller

World Castle Publishing, LLC
Pensacola, Florida
Copyright © 2023 Shein Partnership, LLC
Authors: Erik Daniel Shein, Melissa Davis & Karen Fuller
Hardback ISBN: 9798891260573
Paperback ISBN: 9798891260580
eBook ISBN: 9798891260597
First Edition World Castle Publishing, LLC, October 24, 2023
http://www.worldcastlepublishing.com

Cover: Cover Designs by Karen
https://www.cover-designs-by-karen.com
Editor: Gwyneth Fullerton

Chapter 1

If staring out the window was a pastime, Maddie Tyler had already mastered it as they drove across the country to the bumkin town where her father was dragging them. As she gazed out the car window, Maddie couldn't help but feel a sense of dread creeping up her spine. She had never been a fan of small towns with their close-knit communities and nosy neighbors. She knew that small towns had their own brand of darkness lurking just beneath the surface. Even though it meant she would get to spend the summer with Minnie, Maddie was not looking forward to it.

Sighing impatiently, she tapped her wireless earbuds and skipped to the next song, hoping to tune out the disdain that was pumping through her veins. Would this trip never end? Seventeen, and she felt like half her life had already passed her by, much like the cornfields waving at her outside the window. She shivered as she stared harder at the passing scenery. Were there children in those fields? Were those banjos peeling in the background? She had read enough books and watched enough movies to know that behind the picturesque facade of these towns lay secrets and hidden agendas. Maddie had the distinct impression that she was not going to like her new home one bit. Her parents, though, that might be a different story altogether.

Her mother, Jamie, was sitting with her right leg crossed

over her left. Her shoes were off, showing her pale white skin in the low light. Her hands were fidgeting nervously as she looked out the front windshield. Her caramel hair was pulled back behind her head in a low ponytail with natural waves more accentuated by humidity. Maddie saw the lines on her face, wrinkles that had set in over the past seven years. This move was a chance to start over, but none of that was projected across her face.

Maddie closed her eyes and took a small breath before she looked up at her father, Robert. His middle-aged face was trained on the road ahead of him. She watched his black hands at ten and two on the wheel, the way he had taught her as he prepared her for the time she would drive. Just the two of them, it had been a time to put all the drama and everything else to the side. Maddie wondered if it would ever be the same.

Maddie was almost the perfect mix of her parents. There was just a piece missing, the hole that she would never be able to fill. She twirled a strand of her long, dark, curly hair around her fingertip and watched it spring up in reflex. A nervous reflex she couldn't seem to shake even when she was furious with her parents.

Her mother interrupted the silence. "It's not going to be much further, Maddie."

Maddie rolled her eyes and sighed loudly in irritation, her go-to move to show her disapproval of just about any decision her parents had made in the past few months. "Great."

"Don't roll your eyes, young lady." Her father's voice was a mixture of exhaustion and grit, both of which Maddie knew would be best not to test. When Maddie's eyes darted to the front of the van, where her father was driving, she could see the warning in his eyes in the rearview mirror.

And yet, still, Maddie pushed on and doubled down.

What did she have to lose? They were already going to abandon her for the next month or so. What more could they do? "Sorry, but I'm not a willing participant here."

Maddie crossed her arms and glared out the window. If her eyes were lasers, the glass would have shattered with her focus, another trick she had picked up. Maddie cranked up her music in an attempt to tune out the rest of the world, but she could still hear it no matter how hard she tried.

"Attitude..." Robert corrected her.

"Robert...give her time. None of this has been easy for her."

"I know." Jamie reached over to touch his hand, gripping the arm of his seat.

"It's beautiful out here, isn't it?" her father said in an attempt to change the subject.

Maddie nodded without looking away from the window. She watched as the rain-tinted glass reflected back the scenery outside, making it look like a painting.

Her mother turned around to look at Maddie in the backseat. "Maddie, do you remember the last time we visited your grandma's place?"

Maddie shrugged. "I don't know. It's been a while, and I've never been there without..."

Her mother nodded in understanding. "It won't be the same without Makenna."

Maddie looked away, not wanting to talk about Makenna. She had been gone for only a few weeks, but it felt like an eternity, and the pain of her absence was still too raw for Maddie to talk about, not that either of her parents had done much talking about it. The moment Makenna had been put in the ground was the moment neither one of them seemed able to face the fact that she was gone. Sure, they'd allude to her, but not really talk about her sickness or her final moments, all of which haunted Maddie's waking and dreaming moments.

Her father reached over and held her mother's hand. "Maddie, your grandma loves you very much. We know this will be difficult for you, but she'll be there for you and help you through it, okay?"

Maddie nodded but couldn't bring herself to look at either of her parents. If she did, she'd suffer an emotional cave-in, and all the tears she kept hidden would come crashing out like a tidal wave. She tried to latch onto any other thought in the universe but instead landed on staring at the trees as they zoomed past them, counting them randomly until she'd miss count and start all over again.

The car drove on in silence, and all Maddie could hear was the occasional sniffle from her mother or her father, rubbing her shoulder in reassurance. Maddie tried to block out the two of them as she looked out the window, taking in the scenery and letting her thoughts wander. She thought of Makenna and how much she missed her twin sister. She thought of all the things they had done together when they were younger and all the things they would never do again. She thought of their parents and how they had tried so hard to keep Makenna healthy and safe. She thought of her grandma Minnie and how, even though she had never stayed there longer than a week here or there, she was the closest thing Maddie had to a safe haven right now.

Maddie Tyler rested her forehead against the car window, the glass cold against her skin. She gazed out at the passing scenery, watching the trees, the fields, the sky, and the occasional house, all of them blurring together like a watercolor painting. Even though she had told herself not to cry, the tears coursed down her cheeks, and she reached up and wiped them from her eyes. She had no idea what was awaiting her in the small town of Mellow Creek, but she knew it was time to start a new chapter in her life. She took a deep breath and held it for a moment, then let it out slowly, watching as the rain-tinted glass and the outside world blurred together. She wanted to feel something, anything, but the only emotion she felt was an overwhelming emptiness.

Maddie sighed and shifted in her seat, trying to get comfortable. She was exhausted, but sleep was impossible. Every time she closed her eyes, her mind wandered, and she could only think about Makenna. Maddie could still feel her twin's presence inside the car as if Makenna was sitting in the backseat next to her. Maddie could practically hear her twin's voice, full of life and mischief, telling her it would all be okay.

She knew her parents were mourning her twin sister, Makenna, in their own ways, but with their silence, it felt like they had forgotten about her. Hadn't they? They were pretty much uprooting what was left of their family from the only home all of them had shared together. Were they trying to write Makenna out of their lives completely? Maddie longed for her room back home, the sanctuary she had shared with Makenna for as long as she could remember. The two shared everything there: secrets, dreams, fears, and now it was nothing more than an empty space that Maddie no longer belonged to because her parents decided to start over somewhere else.

Maddie's chest ached with the grief of losing her twin, and she felt a lump in her throat that wouldn't go away. She held back more tears, knowing that if she started to cry, she would have to explain why, and she was too ashamed to admit how she felt. Maddie was an expert at pretending to be strong. She had kept a brave face through it all, her only emotion the bitter anger that seemed to come out in spades anytime her parents backed her into a corner. If she were honest with the world, Maddie was always one step away from a massive tidal wave of tears, but she worked hard to keep them bottled up. Every time she thought of her sister's last moments, she wanted to scream, but her throat was too tight. She felt like she was stuck in some sort of limbo, unable to move forward or back or do anything but exist in the present.

Maddie had never felt so alone, so disconnected from her own life. She felt like a ghost, drifting through an empty space, her only connection to the living world being the occasional glimpse out the car's window. Maddie had no idea what was waiting for her at her grandmother's house, but she knew it couldn't be worse than the loneliness she was currently feeling. She just hoped that when she arrived, she would be able to find some kind of peace.

Chapter 2

The long drive only continued to magnify the boredom of her situation. Maddie now lay curled up in the back of the van, her breathing slow and steady as the vehicle's gentle motion cradled her into a deep sleep, not even penetrated by the outdated music coming out of the van's speakers.

The world outside was a blur of passing trees and distant houses, but within the confines of her dreams, Maddie found herself transported to the sun-drenched shore of a familiar beach to a time and place that was like a second home. Their family had traveled there every summer, taking a few weeks away from Makenna's treatments to give her a small piece of normal. In her dream, it was just Maddie and Makenna on the deserted beach, and while she should have felt isolated and alone, having her sister by her side, even just in a dream, made her feel safe and complete. Maddie never needed anything else.

The dream felt so real that Maddie could feel the hot sand under her toes. The sun bathed her shoulders in its warm glow. The water was cool and inviting as it lapped at her ankles. She breathed it in like it was her own natural paradise and felt herself let go of the stress that had anchored itself to her. It was strange that her dreams were the only place where she could relax.

"Hey, Mads. Check this out!" Makenna called, her

hands deftly sculpting the wet sand into an intricate castle, complete with tiny windows and delicate turrets. Makenna had collected shells and rocks to create mosaic patterns where the windows and doors should be.

"Nice!" Maddie looked up from her work. The turtle's shell was cold and hard beneath Maddie's fingertips as she smoothed over some of the edges. Pinching some of the wet, moldable sand, she made a small hole where one of the eyes would be.

"I think that's your best one yet," Makenna complimented her.

"I dunno. Remember the peacock?" Maddie reminded her.

"A tie, then?" Makenna's smile lit up the world around them. Maddie missed it more than she missed anything else in the world.

"Come on," Makenna said, rising to her feet and grabbing Maddie's hand. "Let's go wash off."

The sisters ran into the sparkling ocean, feeling the cool water envelop their bodies as they washed away the remnants of their sandy creations. They splashed each other gleefully, laughing with the unrestrained joy of youth as if they had no cares in the world. The water danced around them, reflecting the sunlight that bathed the scene in a golden glow.

Suddenly, a rogue wave surged from the depths, crashing over them and dragging them beneath the surface. As Maddie struggled against the pull of the water, she managed to break free. She pushed to the surface, gasping for air as her head broke through the waves. She looked around frantically for her sister but found herself completely alone. Panic filled her to the core as she searched to no avail.

"Makenna?" she called out, her voice barely audible above the relentless crash of the surf. The deafening silence that followed was suffocating, filling her lungs like wet cement. Maddie fell to her knees, her heart pounding in her chest, and screamed at the sky above her, desperate for the comfort of her sister's presence. "Makenna!!!"

But it never came.

In the blink of an eye, her surroundings shifted, and she found herself sitting in a sterile hospital room, holding Makenna's pale, fragile hand. The machines surrounding them beeped and whirred, their electronic voices offering cold comfort as they monitored her sister's fading life. Her parents had gone for a small break, leaving Maddie there to have a moment with her sister that was her own. It was a moment that was burned into her brain.

"Please don't go," Maddie whispered through her tears, praying for some miracle to bring Makenna back to her. "I need you."

As if in response to her plea, the van hit a bump in the road, jolting Maddie from her dream. She awoke with a start, feeling the wetness of her own tears on her cheeks. Silently, she wiped them away with her sleeve, not wanting anyone to see her vulnerability. She stared out the window, her heart heavy with the weight of her loss, as the world continued to rush by in a blur of color and light.

It took a second for Maddie to realize why the van stopped. It turned into a small parking lot. She looked out the window and was almost relieved to see they were finally getting something to eat. "Pizza?"

"If that's all right," answered her mother.

"Better than cheese crackers." Maddie looked down at the remnants of the last box she had annihilated. They were her favorite, but even favorites went out of style after a while. At this point, her stomach realized it was about to get something more nutritious, and it roared its approval with a loud rumbling.

"Someone's hungry," her father added with a smile.

Maddie shrugged as she got out of the van. She knew her parents would give anything for even a feeble smile from her. It just wasn't Maddie's to give right now. It certainly wouldn't absolve them from dumping her in the middle of nowhere, nor would it change the fact that they would be living there for good once her parents got everything resolved back in Maryland. She didn't feel inclined to grant them a reprieve.

Maddie gazed up at the restaurant. From the outside, it was nothing to write home about, just a small building in the middle of nowhere. The only other building nearby was the gas station they would probably stop at after they finished eating. A small sign hung over the door: "Joe's Pizza Shack." A smaller neon sign in the window read "Open" in red letters, inviting them in with its illuminating welcome.

The sign at the front of the restaurant told them to seat themselves, so that was exactly what they did. Her mother picked one of the wooden tables near the window. Maddie pulled one of the wooden chairs out and marveled at how old they appeared, yet sturdy, as she sat down on it. It would never have held up in their household. With twins in the house, their furniture had been banged up, bruised, and broken before it would have ever passed the test of time. They had always been rough and tumble in the early years.

A few minutes after they sat down, an older female waitress came to their table. She placed three menus in front of them. "Can I get you something to drink?"

"Three cokes," ordered Robert.

Maddie picked up the menu and started to look through all the appetizers first. She already knew what they would order. Two pizzas because her parents could never agree on which one to get, and Maddie would end up eating some of each. It was the appetizers where she would find something that was just for her. She settled on beer-battered mushrooms and onion rings.

When the waitress returned with their drinks, she set them carefully in front of them and placed down straws that were still in their paper wrappers. "What can I get you?"

"I want the mushrooms and onion rings," interjected Maddie. She had always been taught to pipe up when she had an order.

"That's my girl," smiled Robert. "We'll need two pizzas too. A large with black olives, and large pepperoni and ham."

"Mixed sampler, pep and ham, and large olive. We'll have this right out for you." The woman scribbled on her notepad and nodded before heading back to the kitchen to put in the order.

While they waited for their food, everyone took that time to scroll through their phones. Maddie checked through her social feed and found her friends back in Maryland were up to their regular antics. Part of her was jealous of how they were moving on with their lives, but the truth was they had already started writing her out long before now. None of them had known how to help her with her losing Makenna. Toward the end, she had felt the bridge between them fading away, while her friends experienced all the joys of life and Maddie learned all the downfalls of death. She couldn't blame them. Her grief could suck all the oxygen out of any room, and they did not want to know what it was like to lose the only tangible breath left.

Blinking, Maddie flicked her finger and closed the feed. Instead, she found a game of solitaire to work her way through. She played a few games before she heard her waitress shuffling toward them. The aroma of hot pizza and melted cheese wafted through the kitchen as the waitress carried the two steaming pies to their table. Maddie's mouth watered at the sight. One was smothered in olives and mushrooms, Jamie's favorite. Her mom loved olives in all shapes and sizes, and truth be told, if green ones had been on the menu, the pizza would have had both on it. The other boasted classic pepperoni and ham, just as Robert liked it.

"I still don't understand how you can eat that monstrosity," Robert teased, pointing at Jamie's olive-laden pizza as it slid on the table in front of them. "Give me a nice, simple pie any day."

Jamie rolled her eyes. "You're such a pizza purist. Live a little!"

"Don't worry, love. Here's Sam with your appetizer right now." The waitress nodded to a teen who placed the basked on the table.

"Thanks."

"You're welcome. Enjoy!"

Maddie reached for the plates on the side of the table and handed one to each of her parents before giving one to herself. She smiled to herself, comforted by her parents' familiar banter. Lately, conversations in the Tyler home had felt heavy, weighted down by discussions of treatments, prognoses, and grief. But for now, listening to her mom and dad bicker lightheartedly about pizza toppings, Maddie could almost pretend everything was normal again.

As they sat down to eat, Robert and Jamie exchanged a look Maddie knew all too well. She tensed, bracing herself for the difficult talk she sensed was coming.

"Your father and I wanted to discuss our plans for the summer," Jamie began gently.

Maddie stared down at her plate, pushing a mushroom through some of the ranch dressing. She'd had a feeling they would be moving ever since Makenna got sick. Still, the reality of leaving her childhood home felt like a punch to the gut. She knew the next few minutes would be the same rehash they had given here at least three times before. Did they think she hadn't listened?

Biting her lip, Maddie listened as her parents explained the job offer, the relocation package, and the temporary stay with Grandma Minnie. She wanted to beg them to stay, to plead for just a little more time in the only town she'd ever known. But one look at their tired, hopeful faces silenced her protests. They were doing what they had to for their family. For her.

As the conversation shifted to lighter topics, the tension in Maddie's shoulders eased. She knew her parents were giving her space to process. Their patience and understanding never failed to amaze her. Gazing around the restaurant, Maddie soaked up the vintage details — the chipped countertops, the faded wallpaper, and the movie memorabilia from times gone past. This was probably a special place to the locals. Maddie would simply remember it as a place they stopped on the way to her summer sentencing. Maddie picked at her pizza crust, her appetite suddenly gone. She knew her parents were watching her, gauging her reaction.

"I know this is hard, sweetie," her dad said gently. "But this job is a great opportunity for us. The insurance company has an excellent reputation."

Maddie just nodded, eyes downcast. She understood why they had to move, but leaving the only home she'd ever known felt like abandoning a piece of herself. Why couldn't they just understand that?

"We'll make sure you get settled with Grandma Minnie before school starts," her mom added. "It's just temporary until we can join you there."

Maddie pictured her parents back home without her. A fresh wave of loss washed over her. She missed her sister so much already; being apart from her parents would make the ache even greater. But Maddie also knew how hard they'd worked since Makenna got sick. How tired and stretched thin they were. This job could give them the fresh start they needed, a time to regroup and find a way to move on with their lives. So she swallowed back the protests rising in her throat. It seemed like a betrayal to move on with life when Makenna would never have a chance to, but that was what they were left with now.

Maddie forced a small smile to her lips. Her parents' relieved expressions made the effort worthwhile. She had to be strong for them. "I know."

Maddie picked at her pizza despite its comforting familiarity. Her parents' animated conversation about the new house they would buy and Robert's exciting job opportunity faded into background noise. All she could think about was everything she'd be leaving behind. Her school, her friends, her childhood home. The memories of Makenna that lived in every corner and crevice. How did they just expect her to leave that all behind without a fight?

She glanced around the pizzeria, taking in the scuffed tiles and was reminded of the mom-and-pop pizzeria back home. She'd come there with her family every Friday night for as long as she could remember. Makenna always got pineapple and ham on her pizza, even though Robert teased her mercilessly for it. Maddie's throat tightened.

Would Makenna fade from her parents' minds in this new life they were building? Would she become just a distant memory, crowded out by new friends and new memories? No, Maddie decided. She wouldn't let that happen. She would keep her twin's spirit alive even if she had to carry Makenna's memory alone. Maddie just had to make sure no one else forgot her either.

Maddie tuned back into her parents' conversation in time to hear Jamie mention looking for a florist job. Maddie smiled softly, picturing her mother's delicate hands arranging flowers again. She had quit her job at the flower shop when Makenna had needed her at home full time. It had always been a creative outlet for her, something in which her mother had also taken pride. Creativity was something she had passed on to both of her daughters.

"We'll make it work," Maddie said suddenly, her voice ringing with determination. Robert and Jamie paused, looking at her in surprise. "As long as we're together, we'll be okay."

Her parents exchanged a relieved look. It was far easier to let them think this would be a cakewalk. Maddie knew it would be anything but. She wasn't about to belay that point at the moment, especially since she was about to be stuck in a van with them for another few hours.

Robert reached across the table and squeezed Maddie's hand. "We'll always be together," he said gently. "No matter where we go, we have each other."

Maddie nodded, blinking back tears. She knew her dad was right, but it still hurt to leave everything familiar behind. Maddie found herself getting caught up in their enthusiasm. Maybe this move wouldn't be so bad. She could reinvent herself at her new school, join clubs, and make new friends. As long as she had her parents, she could face the unknown future with courage.

By the time they polished off the last slices, Maddie felt hopeful. Maybe it was just the feeling of a full stomach, but by the time they made their way back inside the van, Maddie felt a little less like spending every second wallowing in a pit of self-despair. A few more hours and they would finally reach their destination.

Chapter 3

The van rolled to a stop in front of a faded blue house, its white trim peeling from years of harsh weather. Maddie stared out at the sagging porch, overwhelmed with a sense of abandonment as her dad put the van in park. This was it. The beginning of a summer alone with her grandmother in a creaky old house that smelled like mothballs and memories that seemed centuries old.

Maddie stepped reluctantly from the car, the gravel crunching under her sneakers. She caught a glimpse of movement from the corner of her eye. Grandma Minnie emerged slowly from the screen door, her hunched frame supported by a gnarled cane. Maddie swallowed hard against the lump in her throat. Her once vibrant grandmother had withered like a flower deprived of the sun. She had aged even more over the past year, as had all of them.

"Oh, sweet pea, there you are." Grandma Minnie's voice wavered, but her smile glowed warm and comforting. She stretched her free arm toward Maddie.

Maddie went to her grandmother and wrapped her in a gentle embrace, inhaling the faint scent of lavender that still clung to her graying curls. For a moment, the knot in Maddie's chest loosened. She wasn't as alone as she thought.

"I've missed you, honey," Grandma said, patting Maddie's back. "We'll take good care of each other this summer, won't we?"

Maddie nodded, a lump forming in her throat. She hoped they would. Maddie hadn't even realized how much she missed Grandma Minnie until she sunk into her embrace. The comfort reminded her of the first bite of a warm chocolate chip cookie. It just oozed with a warmth that was inexplicable.

Behind them, Maddie's parents were unpacking her bags from the trunk, their voices drifting over.

"I can't believe we're actually doing this," her dad said. "Packing up our whole lives in just a few weeks."

Her mom sighed. "I know. But I really think we all need a fresh start. We'll make new memories in the new house."

Maddie tuned them out, that familiar feeling creeping over her — like she was on the outside looking in ever since Makenna got sick. Her parents kept talking about the move like it was a grand new adventure. But for Maddie, it was just another loss. She fought the urge to say something snarky, to lash out in this moment, but she didn't, mostly because Grandma Minnie didn't deserve that.

She followed her grandmother into the house, the floorboards creaking under them with each step. The living room looked the same as she remembered — chintz sofas, dusty silk flowers, framed photos covering every surface. Minnie never changed her decor. She had always said when a girl knew what she liked, there was no going back. In a way, that was a comfort to come to something so familiar when everything in her life was strange and chaotic.

"I set you up in the lilac room, your favorite," Grandma Minnie said. "Why don't you go get settled?"

Maddie climbed the narrow stairs to the bedroom she always stayed in with her sister when they were little girls. Pale purple walls, white lace curtains, a quilt with faded floral patterns, all things that had appealed to her when she was younger, were not quite what she would have wanted for her room now, but Maddie would bear it for the summer.

She set her bag on the bed and began carefully placing her books on the shelf her favorite stuffed animal on the pillow. Maddie only added a few small touches to make this space feel like her own. Everything else was still back in their house in Maryland. Her mother would be packing it all up, something she refused to let Maddie help with. Maddie had a suspicion that in the packing process, her mom would purge a lot of Makenna's possessions. If Maddie wasn't there, she couldn't put her foot down and stall the process. Maddie didn't blame her. That would totally be her go-to move, but who could blame her. She didn't want them to erase the better half of her life so carelessly.

Maddie headed back downstairs, where she could hear her dad's voice drifting up from the kitchen. His tone was excited. Maddie was surprised to hear him talking about his new pursuits like that. Was he holding back with her?

"It's not the NFL, but I'm excited to work with the high school team," Robert was saying. "I've always loved coaching, and maybe this will open up more opportunities down the line. Even if it's only in an assistant capacity."

"I think it's wonderful, Rob," Grandma Minnie said. "Those boys will be so lucky to have you."

Maddie lingered in the doorway. Her dad's face was lit up with a smile she hadn't seen in months. For the first time, she felt a pang of guilt for being angry at him. He had lost Makenna, too. This was his way of coping.

"What about you, Jamie? Any luck with the florists around town?" Grandma Minnie asked.

Maddie's mom sighed. "I have some interviews next week. I'll be doing online interviews then while I pack up the house. I'm hoping someone needs an extra hand for the next wedding season."

"Well, if anyone knows flowers, it's you," Grandma

Minnie said. She put a gentle hand on Maddie's shoulder. "Remember when you girls used to help your mom arrange bouquets for the church?"

Maddie nodded, transported back to easier times — the scent of gardenias and baby's breath, Makenna giggling as they wove daisies into crowns. That was before the dark cloud had settled over their lives. For the first time since they arrived, the knot in her chest loosened ever so slightly. She was still homesick, still heartbroken. But here, she was with family. She wasn't alone, even though she often felt like she was.

Maddie followed Grandma Minnie into the cozy kitchen, leaving her parents chatting in the living room. The curtains were drawn back to let in the late afternoon sunlight. Outside, the trees swayed gently in the breeze.

"Let's have some tea and talk," Grandma Minnie said, filling the kettle with water.

Maddie sat at the round wooden table. A yellow vase held a small bouquet of wildflowers that perfumed the air with a sweet, earthy scent.

Grandma Minnie eased herself into the chair across from Maddie. Up close, Maddie noticed new lines etched around her grandmother's kind eyes. She was getting older.

"I know this is a difficult time for you," Grandma Minnie said softly. "Losing someone is never easy. But we'll take it one day at a time."

Maddie nodded, tears pricking at the corners of her eyes. "I miss her so much, Grandma."

"I know, sweetheart." Grandma Minnie patted her hand. "But Makenna will always be with you in spirit. And we'll fill this summer with happy memories to hold close to your heart."

The kettle whistled, and Grandma Minnie rose to prepare two mugs of chamomile tea. She placed one in front of Maddie, the fragrant steam wreathing her face. "Now tell me, what shall we do this summer?"

Maddie sipped her tea. For the first time in weeks, she felt a spark of something she thought was lost forever — hope. Maddie took a deep breath and tried to gather her thoughts.

"Well," she began slowly, "I'm excited to spend the summer here with you. But I'm also really nervous about the move. I've never lived anywhere but my hometown."

Grandma Minnie nodded understandingly. "Change can be scary. But just think of all the new adventures waiting for you."

"I know," Maddie said. "It's just...hard to leave everything behind. All my friends and memories with Makenna." Her voice caught on her sister's name.

Grandma Minnie reached over and squeezed Maddie's hand. "You'll make new friends. And you'll carry Makenna with you always."

Maddie dabbed at her eyes with a napkin. "You're right. I know I'll like living here. It's just different, that's all."

"Different can be good," Grandma Minnie said gently.

Just then, the screen door creaked open, and Maddie's parents entered the kitchen. Her dad set down a box labeled "Maddie's Room."

"I'll take this up," he said, wiping his brow. "We'll be heading back first thing tomorrow."

Maddie's mom sighed. "I can't believe how many memories this house holds."

Her voice trailed off sadly. Maddie's dad put an arm around her shoulder. "I know, hon. And there's time for more, too. New ones."

Maddie stayed quiet, swirling the tea in her cup. She knew her parents were trying to move on, too, in their own way. Maybe Grandma Minnie was right. Change could be scary, but it could also lead to new adventures. She just had to be brave enough to find out.

Maddie nodded slowly. "I think I'll take a walk around town before dinner. Might as well start exploring."

Grandma Minnie's eyes crinkled with a smile. "That's the spirit. There's a nice park just down the street."

Maddie stood, gave her grandma a quick hug, and headed for the front door. Stepping outside, she took a deep breath of the fresh summer air. The sidewalk was lined with tall oak trees that cast dappled shadows on the ground.

As she strolled along, Maddie noticed a group of teenagers laughing and chatting on a front porch up ahead. She felt a pang, remembering her friends back home. Maybe she'd meet people here, too, she thought. She just had to put herself out there.

The park came into view, an expanse of green grass and flowerbeds. Maddie wandered over to a bench beneath a willow tree. Its long, trailing branches created a sheltered little nook. She sat for a while, watching kids play on the playground while parents looked on. The laughter and shouts mingled with birdsong in the air. Despite her sadness, Maddie felt the tiniest spark of anticipation. This place was new and unfamiliar, but it also held possibilities. Adventures she couldn't even imagine yet.

As the sunlight faded, Maddie headed back to Grandma Minnie's, feeling just a little lighter. This summer would be full of changes, but she was ready to embrace them.

Chapter 4

Later that night, Maddie was having trouble sleeping when everyone else had gone to sleep. So she did what any average teen would do: she tiptoed downstairs and let herself out the back door. She didn't know where she was headed, only that she was being pulled a particular way. Maybe it was the moon, or the way the fireflies danced magically around her, or just the teenage rebellion that was already stirring in her heart as Maddie headed away from the house.

The full moon cast an eerie glow over the overgrown field behind Grandma Minnie's house as she crept through the tall grass. The chirping crickets were deafening but not loud enough to drown out the pounding of her heart. The fireflies played peekaboo through the long blades, calling to their mates in the darkness.

She hadn't been back here since the last time she and Makenna had snuck out. That had been at least three years ago. Tonight, the pain of her sister's absence felt sharper than ever, but in this moment, there was a small promise of peace if she could just find the one place she felt reminded her the most of her twin. She needed to feel close to Makenna again, even if just for a moment.

Maddie's eyes found the old oak tree, its limbs like crooked fingers clawing at the night sky. She and Makenna used to spend hours climbing that tree, whispering secrets and dreaming up adventures, mostly the ones that involved finding the secret treasure that Grandma Minnie always told them about every summer. She ran her fingers over the rough bark and pulled herself up onto the first branch, just like she had so many times before.

Up and up, Maddie climbed, the exertion making it impossible to dwell on her grief. This was the closest she had felt to her sister in weeks. If she closed her eyes, she could almost imagine Makenna right there beside her. But when Maddie reached their favorite perch and looked over, there was no one. Just an empty space where her twin should have been. Her breath caught in her throat as the pain came flooding back.

"I miss you so much, Kenna," she whispered into the night.

What would Makenna say to her if she were here now? Tell her about the bank robbers who had hidden out in the caverns of Mellow Creek. There was no truth to the stories, really. How could there be? The caverns had been closed off years ago. Everyone knew how treacherous they were. Makenna's theory had always been that the thieves had burrowed deeper inside and set up a small camp in the darkness. She had always been a dreamer. They both had. Dreams weren't reality, though. They were unproven, unsteady, unsure.

She wasn't sure how long she sat up there. Maddie was staring at the spot next to her for so long, as if doing so would conjure the one thing she wanted to see most in the world. Tears were streaming down her cheeks, her eyes way of protecting them from her lack of blinking. Eventually, Maddie knew she had to climb back down and face the world again — a world without her other half.

Maddie wiped the tears from her cheeks and steeled herself for the descent. As she turned to start climbing down, a flicker of light caught her eye. She looked up to see fireflies dancing all around her, their glow soft and warm. Maddie gasped as she noticed one firefly in particular that hovered right next to her, its light pulsing gently.

"Kenna?" she whispered in disbelief.

The firefly bobbed lightly as if nodding in response. Maddie's heart swelled, and she reached out her hand slowly. The firefly landed right on her fingertip, its glow enveloping her in comfort. In that moment, Maddie knew her sister was still with her, if only in spirit. The crushing sorrow she had felt just moments before melted away, replaced by a sense of peace.

"I love you, Kenna," Maddie said softly. "I always will."

The firefly flickered once more before floating up and away, blending in with the others. Maddie watched it go, a bittersweet smile on her face. She took a deep breath and began her descent, holding on to the feeling of closeness with her sister, the one sign she had desperately needed.

She moved slowly, carefully placing her feet on the knobs and grooves worn smooth from years of use. About halfway down, her foot slipped. Maddie gasped, scrambling for purchase on the rough bark. Her heart lurched as she started to fall, but she managed to catch herself on a branch. She clung there, breathing hard. After a moment, the panic subsided. Maddie steadied herself and continued descending, more cautious than before.

When Maddie reached the ground, she turned back for one last glimpse of the oak tree. The fireflies still danced between its branches, a reminder that even death could not break the bond between sisters. Maddie took a step away from the oak tree, ready to make her way back home through the moonlit field. Suddenly, a figure emerged from the shadows near the tree, causing Maddie to gasp and stumble backwards.

Tristen Grant. He had certainly changed over the years. At first, Maddie had trouble recognizing him because the last time she had seen him, he was freckle-faced and in braces. He had certainly grown into something that barely even resembled the awkward boy down the road. His messy blonde hair fell over his forehead as he stood there smirking, the moonlight glinting off his black leather jacket. But it was his piercing blue eyes that unnerved Maddie the most, staring right through her with an intensity that made her skin prickle.

"Well, well, if it isn't little Maddie Tyler," Tristen drawled, sauntering towards her. "What are you doing out here this late?"

"That's none of your business," she said, trying to keep her voice steady. Maddie's heart pounded, her mind racing. She hadn't expected anyone else to be out here tonight. "Just leave me alone."

"Whoa, hold on. Are you all right?" His words seemed genuine. He took another step closer to Maddie, invading her space.

"Where did you come from?" Maddie stood frozen, warring with herself. Part of her wanted to run, but she refused to show weakness to Tristen. She lifted her chin defiantly, meeting his gaze.

"There's a party two fields down, by the pond. Just a small shindig."

"Maybe you should just get back to it then and leave me alone," she said.

Tristen raised an eyebrow, looking vaguely annoyed with her. For a moment, neither of them moved. The sound of crickets and rustling leaves filled the tense silence. Finally, Tristen shrugged and stepped back. "Fine," he said with a smirk. "I was just leaving anyway."

He turned and sauntered away, the darkness quickly swallowing his figure. Maddie let out a shaky breath, her adrenaline crashing. She cast one last glance at the oak tree before hurrying home, eager to escape this unexpected encounter.

Maddie had only taken a few steps when she heard giggling coming from the direction Tristen had gone. She paused, squinting into the darkness. Two shadowy figures emerged from behind a corpse of trees. Tristen with what Maddie could only assume was one of the cheer squad leaders. It was the high ponytail and booty shorts that gave it away.

Maddie's stomach twisted. Of course, he was with someone like her. She was probably the head cheerleader, and what was he now, the quarterback, a perfect I couple. The assumption wasn't too far off, considering how much pressure Trent's father put on him during peewee football. Why did it irritate Maddie so much how radiant his date looked in the moonlight, as her long blonde hair swirled around her shoulders while she laughed at something Tristen said?

They were walking close together, the girl clinging to Tristen's arm. She'd have to be one of those girls who latched onto her prey and never let go. A leech, more than likely.

"Oh my gosh, did you see her face, Tristen?" Tiffany said with a giggle, spotting Maddie. "She looked so shocked, like a little mouse caught in a trap."

"Tiffany, be nice. She wasn't expecting to see anyone out here," Tristen admonished.

"She looks like a little goody-two-shoes. What would her daddy say if he knew she was out past her curfew?"

"Probably the same as yours, Tiff."

"He'd have to catch me first." Tiffany laughed louder this time. "What's she doing here, anyway?"

"I don't know. Maybe she's visiting for the summer. What do I care?" answered Tristen.

The pair of them started to walk away, and Maddie

heard them laugh again. They were probably laughing at her again. Maddie felt her face burn with humiliation. She wanted to shout at them, but she bit her tongue. It wasn't worth engaging. Maddie stood there for a moment longer, shaking. The night air, which had felt so peaceful before, now seemed suffocating. She glanced up at the oak tree, its limbs swaying gently in the breeze. Only minutes ago, she'd felt close to Makenna here. Now, the tree seemed cold and empty.

The tall grass swished around her legs as she walked, wet with dew. Overhead, the full moon was bright and watchful. Maddie kept her arms wrapped around herself as she moved through the silvery darkness. Part of her wanted to run, to get back to the safety of home as fast as she could. But each step was heavy, weighed down by anger and fear and grief.

She thought of the concern in Tristen's eyes moments before that girl Tiffany had shown up. She thought of the way that girl had sized her up with her snobby little eyes. And she thought of Makenna, whose spirit she'd felt so close just minutes before. Now, even that comfort seemed lost to her. Tristen and Tiffany had ruined that.

Maddie swiped at the tears that slid down her cheeks. She felt so alone out here in this wide, empty field. But she kept walking, putting one foot in front of the other until she reached the fence at the edge of her yard. With a deep breath, Maddie headed for the house. She moved quietly up the porch steps and slipped inside, leaving the moonlit field behind.

Inside, the lights in the living room were on, harsh and bright compared to the soft moonlight outside. Maddie froze in the entryway, her heartbeat quickening. Her father sat waiting on the couch, his face set in hard lines. He looked up as Maddie came in, and she saw the anger simmering in his eyes.

"Where have you been?" he demanded, his voice

booming in the quiet house.

Maddie shrank back against the door. "I just...went for a walk. I couldn't sleep."

"A walk?" Her father stood up. "Do you have any idea what time it is? Sneaking out in the middle of the night!"

He came toward Maddie, arms crossed over his broad chest. She could feel his disappointment and worry radiating off him in waves. "I'm sorry, Dad, I—"

"You could've been hurt, or kidnapped, or worse!" he interrupted. "What were you thinking, Maddie? After everything we've already been through?"

"I'm sorry," she said again, her voice small. Maddie's throat tightened. She knew he was thinking of Makenna. They all were, every day, every minute.

Her dad's face softened slightly, but his jaw was still tense. "You can't keep acting recklessly like this. There are rules for a reason."

Maddie stared down at the floor, tears burning her eyes again. She heard footsteps and looked up to see her mom coming down the stairs in her robe.

"What's going on down here?" she asked gently. She put a hand on Maddie's shoulder and glanced between her and her husband. "Let's all just take a breath, okay? We don't want to wake Minnie up."

"How are we going to be able to trust you here, Maddie?" Robert looked over at Jamie. "Maybe Mom shouldn't be in charge of her. It might be too much for her to handle."

"I'll have you know I have a lot of kick left in me," Grandma Minnie interrupted from the middle of the stairs. "The girl took a walk, Rob. Not much different than what you used to do, and you turned out just fine."

"Things are different now, Mom. The world is not like it used to be." Robert turned to look at his daughter. "You can't take risks, Maddie."

"I won't," whispered Maddie. Her bottom lip trembled, and tears threatened to pour down her face.

"Let the poor child get to bed, Rob." Grandma Minnie's voice wasn't so soft this time. Instead, it was stern, a mother talking to her own child. "I can handle a teenage girl. You don't have to worry about me."

"Minnie's right." Jamie put her hand on Robert's arm. "Let's get some sleep. We have a long drive ahead of us tomorrow. Maddie will be fine here. She has a good head on her shoulders, Rob."

"I used to think so," muttered Robert.

Maddie stiffened on the stairs at his dig. There had been many over the past year. Maddie tried to stuff it inside with the rest of them, but this one hurt more than the rest. She forced herself to put one foot in front of the other as she climbed the stairs.

When she reached the room, she kicked off her shoes and stepped closer to the bed. As she lay down, she pulled the comforter over her. The bed was warm and comfortable; the sheets were smooth and silky beneath her. As she sunk into them, the small click of the fan overhead reminded her of a soft breeze on her bare arms. She shut her eyes and let her thoughts roam as she drifted off to sleep.

Chapter 5

Tristen shrugged off his leather jacket. The night air wasn't nearly as cold next to the large campfire. He tossed it on an overturned log nearby and sat down next to it. Tristen's gaze was mesmerized by the shifting patterns of orange, yellow and red in the campfire. The sounds of music and laughter started to melt into the night as if they had been consumed by the flames.

He should be having fun right now, enjoying one of their summer heyday parties. But instead, all he could think about was the tense conversation with his dad right before he left for the bonfire.

"I better see recruiters from State and Tech this year," his dad had said, his voice cold and hard. "No son of mine is going to play for some no-name college."

Tristen swallowed hard, his throat tight. He knew how much his dad wanted him to play for a top college program, to follow in the footsteps of Daniel Grant, a local football legend. Well, half in his footsteps, for his dad had never made it to the college part. Something Tristen had never heard the end of growing up. This time would be better. This time, Tristen would do what his father hadn't been able to do. All his father's hopes and dreams rested on Tristen's shoulder.

But the truth was, Tristen didn't even know if he wanted to play college ball. Lately, he had been feeling suffocated by his dad's expectations, wishing he could just enjoy playing high school football without the pressure of performing for scouts and living up to the Grant name.

Tristen stared down at his shoes. What he wouldn't give to be able to outrun his father's expectations. If only he had the courage to break free from what his father wanted for him. He could feel the nervous energy inside him, ready to run from his obligations and fulfill his own dreams for a change. But no matter how much he wanted it, he was still too afraid of disappointing the one person he didn't want to let down.

He thought about Maddie Tyler and wondered If she had the same expectations on her shoulders. Tristen had read the obituary in the paper. Everyone here in Mellow Creek had known about Makenna's death. Was that the unbearable weight of sorrow he saw behind her glossy brown eyes? A crushing burden that seemed to reach out and wrap its inky tentacles around her, and he could see it stifling the air from her lungs as if her every breath hurt. One glance and Tristen felt as if he could see into her soul. He had never had an instant connection with any other girl.

A petite hand grasped Tristen's arm, jolting him from his thoughts. Tiffany gazed up at him, her green eyes pleading beneath her expertly curled blonde hair. "Let's dance," she said brightly, giving his arm a tug.

Tristen opened his mouth, but no words came out. The pulsing music pounded in his ears. All he could see was the disappointment in his dad's eyes. It was scorched into the forefront of his mind. Tiffany's hopeful smile faded as Tristen turned and pushed her hand away. "Just stop."

Tristen watched Tiffany huff off, her face flushed with embarrassment. She walked with a light spring in her step, but Tristen could feel the weight of his words pressing down on her. They had already fought twice today, and he knew this was not the last battle they were going to have. Why did she have to be so needy all the time?

Tiffany walked over to her circle of friends. "Well, this wasn't how tonight was supposed to go at all."

"Tell me about it, girl," added Sara. "What's with Tristen?"

"I dunno. Another mood swing, I guess."

"Men and their testosterone," shrugged Sara.

"Yeah, sure," Tiffany answered half-heartedly.

"There's plenty of other choices here." Sara gestured to the group of teens around them. "Maybe a little green-eyed monster will bring him around?"

"Tristen, jealous? I'm not sure he has a jealous bone in his body." Tiffany sighed. "I guess it can't hurt, though."

Tiffany grabbed Sara's hand and started to wiggle them closer to a group of football players who were conversing a little further from the fire. "Wanna dance with us?" Sara asked.

It only took a few seconds for the boys to turn their attention to the two girls. Every now and then, the girls took turns looking back at Tristen to see what his reaction would be. He watched them with little interest, for his mind was not in the moment. It was in the past, and every conversation his father had driven into his head the past four years.

"That's it, boys, we don't bite. Much..." Tiffany's voice called loud enough to make sure Tristen heard her. The girls hooted and hollered, hyping her up.

Tristen met her eyes and sighed. They would have to talk this out, or she would continue to make a spectacle of herself. Tristen's body uncoiled from the log, his muscles flexing in the firelight as he strode closer with intent. His eyes remained locked on Tiffany, determined and unwavering, as he made his way to her.

"Here he comes," Sara said under her breath.

"About time," muttered Tiffany.

"Want me to say something to him?" Sara asked protectively.

"No, it's okay." Tiffany squared her shoulders. "I'll handle this."

As the other girls hung back, Tiffany approached Tristen alone. He glanced up as she neared.

"Hey," he said neutrally.

"Hey." Tiffany crossed her arms. "Are you enjoying completely ignoring me tonight?"

Tristen winced. "Look, I'm sorry. I just have a lot on my mind."

"Yeah, clearly," Tiffany said sarcastically.

An uncomfortable silence fell. Tristen shifted his weight, shoving his hands in his pockets.

"Do you even want to be here with me?" Tiffany finally burst out.

Tristen met her eyes for the first time all night. "Of course I do," he said softly. "It's just...things with my dad have been bad lately. The family business..."

He trailed off, but Tiffany could read the stress in his face. Her expression softened.

"I'm here for you, Tristen," she said gently. "You can talk to me."

Tristen nodded, his eyes glistening. Tiffany stepped forward and wrapped her arms around him. After a moment, she felt his body relax as he hugged her back.

Tristen held Tiffany tight, taking comfort in her embrace. But despite his best efforts to stay focused on the present, his thoughts kept wandering back to the ceaseless troubles with his dad. A subtle tug of guilt weighed heavily on him as he struggled to make sense of the complicated relationship between them. He desperately wanted for things to go back to how they used to be but knew that would take a miracle.

Why did it have to be this way? Why couldn't his dad just let him be his own person? Ever since he could remember, his dad had been grooming him to either play college ball or take on a job at the car lot. But Tristen's passion was football, not selling policies.

He thought back to earlier that evening when his dad had laid into him again about focusing on his future instead of "playing games." The constant criticism and demands were exhausting. Tristen felt like he was being pulled in two directions: his own dreams versus his family legacy. If only his dad could understand that just because they shared the same last name didn't mean Tristen had to follow the same path. He wasn't a carbon copy of his father. Tristen had his own hopes, his own talents. All he wanted was the freedom to pursue them without the weight of expectations.

But he knew his dad would never bend. It had to be his way or no way. The Grant family name came before all else. Tristen sighed, his breath ruffling Tiffany's hair. She looked up at him quizzically. He wished he could tell her everything he was feeling, but he didn't want to burden her with his family issues. She just wouldn't understand. To her, having any kind of relationship was a matter of status in high school. Tristen didn't really care for all the drama that went along with all of that. Was it even necessary?

For now, Tristen resolved to keep his chin up. He still had football, still had a chance at a future beyond his dad's control. As long as he kept his focus, he could get through this. He could use the one sport he hated to get out of here and never look back if he chose to. A means to an end, that's all it was.

Tristen gently pulled back from the hug and offered a consolatory smile down at Tiffany, hoping to keep her questions at bay. "Thanks," he said. "I needed that."

Tristen relaxed when he saw her smile up at him. The tension between them started to dissipate. He was thankful that she wasn't delving in any deeper. He wasn't sure he wanted to go into more details at the moment. Tristen wished he had an off button for all the worries he held inside him. That would certainly make life easier. Weren't men supposed to shut off their emotions and pretend they didn't exist? That was the status quo, right? The truth was that was a lie. Men had emotions. They had fears just like anyone else. Tristen was tired of pretending they didn't exist in order to be some kind of macho man.

"Time to relax and forget yourself." Tiffany squeezed Tristen's hand reassuringly as they walked back to the campfire. The party was in full swing — music blasting, people dancing and shouting to be heard over the din.

Tristen tried to push his conflicted thoughts about his dad out of his mind and live in the moment. But his eyes kept drifting to the window, towards the direction of his house. He wondered what his dad was doing right now. Probably still at the office, even though it was nearly midnight. Daniel Grant didn't believe in rest, only results. Tristen sighed, his shoulders slumping. Tiffany glanced up at him, eyebrows knitted in concern.

"You okay?" she asked.

Tristen paused, debating how to answer. He didn't want to lie, but he also didn't feel ready to open up. It was easier to just let it be, but sometimes people just wouldn't give him that head space.

"I'm alright," he finally said. "Just tired."

Tiffany studied his face. Tristen could tell she knew there was more to it than that. But she didn't push, thankfully. Thank goodness for small favors.

"Do you want to get out of here?" she asked. "We could go for a drive, look at the stars?"

Tristen hesitated. Part of him wanted to say yes, to escape with Tiffany into the peaceful night, but they had already tried a moonlit stroll to do just that and failed. Although part of him wondered if they would run into Maddie again. That would have been worth wandering back into the fields again, but somehow, he didn't think Tiffany would appreciate that much.

"I think I'm gonna stick around a little longer," Tristen said. "But raincheck on the drive?"

Tiffany nodded, though her eyes were tinged with disappointment. "Sure, whenever you're ready," she said softly.

She stood on her tiptoes to kiss his cheek. Then, with a small, sad smile, she turned and disappeared into the crowd, leaving Tristen alone with his thoughts once more. He was thankful for the solitude.

Chapter 6

Maddie looked warily at her parents as they stood over her bed. She had been dreading this moment for months since her parents had announced that the family was moving to Alabama. She had expected it to be hard, but now that the day of their departure had arrived, Maddie was feeling an overwhelming sense of sadness and fear. The air was heavy with tension, and Maddie's heart felt like a weight in her chest, sinking deeper and deeper with each passing second. No one was doing anything to make her feel any better in this moment. Did they not understand how hard this was for her?

"Well, I think it's time," her dad said, trying to keep his voice even. "We have a long drive ahead of us."

Maddie nodded and rose from her bed, her dad and mom leading the way from her room. As they walked, Maddie kept glancing back at the hallway, imagining her sister standing quietly against the wall. At least Maddie would have her memory to keep her company. It wasn't like she'd have her parents to help her navigate the next few months. Did they think she was over her sister's death already? It had only been a few months out of a lifetime she'd shared with someone who had been more than a sister to her. Makenna was half of her soul, and Maddie was lost without her. How could they be so blind to it all?

As they walked down the stairs, Maddie could hear

her parents discussing their plans for the future, but she couldn't seem to focus on anything other than the sadness that was slowly filling her heart. It was suffocating. With each step down the stairs, Maddie felt the wood would swallow her whole, sinking into them like some wooden quicksand that would make her disappear into nothingness. Help me, she wanted to scream at them. Don't leave me too...Take me with you. All of it circled in her head, but none of it left her lips. Instead, Maddie clenched her teeth together, squared her shoulders and pretended for the millionth time this year that everything was A-okay.

When they stepped out onto the front porch of Grandma Minnie's house, Maddie was surprised to see that her grandmother had already been out doing her gardening. She looked up and waved at Maddie and her parents, her smile gentle and kind. Grandma Minnie's white hair was pulled back in a bun, and her petite frame was dressed in her usual gardening clothes—a light-colored dress with a straw hat covering her face. She was on her knees in the dirt, weeding around a small flower bed with a smile on her face as she waved at Maddie and her parents.

Maddie's mom put an arm around her shoulders and said, "I know this isn't easy, Maddie. Just try and get through. We'll be back before you know it, and we'll start our new life here."

Maddie wanted to argue with them, wanted to throw herself on the ground like a toddler and throw a massive tidal wave of a tantrum, but she just couldn't do it. She had learned to be strong, solid like an old oak, unbending and stuck in the mold she had held herself in the whole time her sister was sick. Stay strong, Maddie. Don't cry, Maddie. Makenna needs you, Maddie. Apparently, the mold had taken root so tight that Maddie couldn't shake free from it. So, instead of rebelling, she did the only thing she had trained herself to do.

She put all her thoughts and feelings aside.

Maddie hugged her parents tightly, trying to soak in every moment, every detail of them. She could feel her mom's hair brushing her face and the warmth of her dad's embrace. It broke through the icy barrier around her heart, and for once, she was reminded that her parents loved her. It calmed her soul just enough to help her get through.

"It's going to be alright, Maddie," her mom said, pushing her back and looking into her eyes. "We'll be checking in with you throughout the summer. We love you, and we'll never be too far away."

Maddie nodded, trying to hold back her tears. Her dad wrapped his arms around both of them and said, "We'll miss you lots, sweetheart."

Maddie nodded again, not trusting herself to speak. She hugged them both one last time and watched as her parents turned and walked down the sidewalk. Saying goodbye to her parents had been harder than Maddie thought it would be. She stood on the porch, watching them get into their van and drive away, feeling like she was no longer a part of her own family. She took a deep breath, fighting off tears. How could it be so easy for them to just drive off and leave her there? Was it just as easy for them to pack every inch of Makenna away, too?

Trying to fight off the anguish inside was becoming a losing battle. Maddie could only be so strong for so long. Her exterior was cracking as her emotions tried to crash through her resolve. Just a little longer, she reminded herself as she stood up straighter and attempted to rally more strength from somewhere inside her.

Her mother leaned out the window and called back to her, "Everything will be OK! We love you!"

Grandma Minnie put her arm around Maddie's shoulders and said, "Stay here, sweetheart. I'll make some tea, and we'll make some plans to get you out of the house today."

Maddie followed her, a mix of sadness and anticipation bubbling inside her. Even though she was scared of the unknown, Maddie knew that she was going to make the most of her summer and that her parents would always be just a phone call away. She would just have to make the best of this situation, no matter how crumby it appeared. At least she'd have Grandma Minnie to keep her company.

A few moments later, the two of them were sitting on the front porch of Grandma Minnie's house, a modest but warm and inviting two-story in the middle of the small town of Mellow Creek. They were drinking sweet tea and watching the world quietly continue about its day. Grandma Minnie had lived there most of her life with Grandpa James, who had passed away several years ago. Maddie barely remembered him, but Minnie always had wonderful stories to share, most about her father when he was a young boy.

Grandma Minnie looked out at the horizon, beyond the rooftops of the town, and told Maddie a little more about Mellow Creek. "It's a cozy little place. Quaint and charming. You'll love it here, Maddie. You just need to give it a chance."

"But what if I'm a city girl?" Maddie asked.

"That will change, you'll see." Grandma Minnie said. "How about we head into town? We can explore the shops, have lunch, and just take in the scenery. What do you say?"

Maddie wasn't delighted by her circumstances here, but she could make the best of it. Besides, she loved to spend time with Grandma Minnie. "Makenna and I used to go there a lot when we were kids, but it's been a while. I think it sounds like a great plan."

Grandma Minnie smiled and clapped her hands. "Wonderful! We can leave as soon as we're done with tea."

Not much later, Grandma Minnie and Maddie set

out on the journey to Mellow Creek. It only took a matter of minutes to get there. The town was right up the road, after all. Along the way, Grandma Minnie described the quaint shops, the old-fashioned ice cream parlor, and the scenic walking trails. Her words were enough for Maddie to conjure memories from years gone by, where she had eaten ice cream with Grandma Minnie and Makenna after an afternoon stroll through the town.

When they arrived in Mellow Creek, Maddie was taken aback by the town's beauty, as if seeing it for the first time all over again. The streets were lined with old-fashioned lamp posts and charming shops. The architecture had elaborately painted facades and wrought iron balconies. It really took her back to another time and place, like history was coming alive.

Grandma Minnie and Maddie made their way down the main street, stopping to admire the various stores and small businesses. Maddie was especially delighted by the old-fashioned ice cream parlor, with its bright awnings and sweet treats. It had barely changed since the last time Maddie had been there. That was the comforting thing about small towns; they rarely changed. That was one thing she could count on to be steady in her life here. Slow town, easy living. Maybe it wouldn't be so bad here after all.

When lunchtime came, Grandma Minnie and Maddie stopped at a small bistro called the I on the corner of the town square. They enjoyed a delicious lunch of homemade soup and sandwiches, and Maddie was enchanted by the I's cozy atmosphere and homey feel. It was definitely tastier than the fast food restaurants she had gotten used to eating at over the past year. At first, when Makenna was sick this last time, there was a food train that brought food to their house. Every night, a different dish from a different family. Maddie had never realized how many people they had known until all the food had started pouring into the house. After a while, that fizzled out as the treatment wore on longer than they expected. Maddie didn't understand at the time why people had suddenly stopped caring, but it wasn't that. Generosity had its limits. People had to take care of their own, too. Then, when it had gotten closer to the end, people were almost afraid to offer help or send anything.

What did you say to a family that was losing a child? No one wanted to imagine how horrific it was. Maddie understood. She hadn't wanted to live through it either. It would have been easier if Makenna had taken her with her. Closing her eyes, Maddie tried to push that thought deep down. Now was not the time for a mental breakdown. It would only make Grandma Minnie worry, and she didn't want to ruin their afternoon outing.

After lunch, Grandma Minnie decided it was time to let Maddie do her own exploration of the town. "You remember how to get back home?"

"Yes. Besides, I have this," Maddie held up her phone. "It's hard to get lost when you have built-in maps."

"Be smart and have fun, young lady." Grandma Minnie tapped her on the nose with her finger and smiled at her.

The church bells tolled in the distance as Maddie made her way down Main Street, taking in the sights of the quaint small town around her. Red brick storefronts lined the cobblestone road, window boxes bursting with colorful flowers. An old-fashioned barbershop pole spun lazily in front of the corner barber as a few locals chatted on a bench outside.

Maddie tucked a strand of hair behind her ear, her shoes pounding softly on the uneven stones. She breathed in the faint scent of lilacs on the breeze, and for the first time in a few hours, she was reminded of the hole that would never be filled. Makenna had always loved the scent of lilacs. One thought and the ache that constantly gripped her heart almost toppled her. She missed her sister fiercely — her laugh, her fiery spirit, the way she knew Maddie better than anyone else. Each day without her was its own slow torture. And it never stopped. It was like the earth opened up and swallowed her whole every time grief rose to the surface. Makenna would always be the hole in her sky, the missing piece she'd never find again: her oxygen. Makenna didn't know how to survive in a world without her. She could barely breathe without her.

A butterfly flitted in front of her, and Maddie was momentarily distracted by its beauty. In that instant, she found her sister's smile, her calming touch as the butterfly landed on her nose for a brief second before fluttering away. The wonders of nature and color that's where Makenna survived around her. Maddie took a deep breath and recentered herself. She needed to learn to stay in the moment.

As Maddie wandered past the quirky antique shops and bakeries, she felt like a ghost drifting through a world that no longer made sense. She stuck out like a sore thumb in her plain t-shirt and jeans while the locals smiled and waved cheerfully at one another. No one knew of the gaping hole inside her or how hard it was just to get out of bed each morning. Or did they? Every once in a while, Maddie could see a pitying glance, and it made her feel like jumping out of her skin. How many people knew about Makenna?

Maddie paused outside the bookshop, its display window crammed with leather-bound volumes. Makenna would have loved this place, spending hours getting lost in the stacks. She could practically hear her twin's voice urging her to go inside and explore, to find something that sparked joy again. Maddie took a deep breath. She wasn't ready, not yet — but maybe someday. For now, it was enough just to be here, taking in the sights and sounds of a world full of life.

As Maddie turned to continue her aimless stroll down Main Street, the door to the nearby art store swung open. A tall teen with messy blonde hair stepped out, carefully balancing a canvas in his hand and a shopping bag in the other.

"Oh, sorry!" The teen said with an easy smile as he dodged around her.

The fog cleared, and Maddie clawed her way back to the present. What had she just been thinking about? Where was she going? It was then that she realized that she had almost plowed right into Tristen Grant. Maddie blurted the first thing that came to mind. "No problem. Sorry, Tristen"

"Maddie," he replied. He had a nice voice – smooth and reassuring.

An awkward beat passed. Maddie struggled for something else to say. Her twin would have known exactly how to keep the conversation going, how to be effortlessly charming. Makenna would probably have picked up right where they had left off the last time they had seen each other. What were they doing then? Hide and seek? Makenna had been the best hider. She could always get into small spaces, even though they were the same size. Maddie had often teased her that she would be a good contortionist if she ever wanted to run off and join the circus.

"Are you visiting town?" Tristen asked curiously.

Maddie shook her head. "No, my parents are moving us here. Or they will be. For now, I'm staying with my grandma."

"How are you liking it so far?"

She thought about the quaint storefronts and friendly residents. It was picturesque in a way that felt foreign to her like a postcard come to life. "It's different but nice, I think. Quieter than I'm used to."

"It's definitely a change of pace. But as you already know, I grew up here, but I don't take the peacefulness for granted." He smiled, his eyes crinkling at the corners. "Once you settle in, I'd be happy to show you some of my favorite local spots."

"What about Tiffany?" Maddie was sure that Tiffany would have something to say about that. She seemed like the jealous type.

"What about her?" asked Tristen.

"You seemed to be quite the pair last night," Maddie pointed out.

"Oh, that. We're not, not really." Tristen shrugged off her words.

Maddie's heart fluttered again. Was he single? "Well, in that case, I think I'd like that."

They exchanged numbers, both shy but eager. As Tristen waved and continued on his way, Maddie found herself looking forward to exploring the town with him. For the first time since losing Makenna, she felt a spark of hope. Maddie watched Tristen walk away, his figure getting smaller as he made his way down the cobblestone street. She could still feel the butterflies fluttering wildly in her stomach, her heart racing as she replayed their interaction in her mind.

She hadn't expected to meet someone like him so soon after arriving in this sleepy little town. Let alone have an instant connection that left her palms sweaty and her cheeks flushed. But there was something different about Tristen – something that drew her to him like a magnet. Maybe it was because they had a history together, one that they shared with Makenna. Maddie knew her twin would have approved. Makenna was always telling her to open up, to let new people in, instead of closing herself off from the world.

"What do you have to lose?" Makenna would say. "Just put yourself out there."

With Tristen, Maddie finally felt brave enough to take that advice. She could practically hear Makenna's voice cheering her on, telling her to text him and make plans to hang out soon. For once, that thought of Makenna wasn't mixed with dread and despair.

Maddie took a deep breath and steadied her nerves before pulling out her phone. Her fingers trembled slightly as she composed a message to Tristen: "Hey! Nice Meeting U. Luv 2 get coffee sometime."

She hit send before she could overthink it, then slid her phone back into her pocket, a shy smile spreading across her face. Whatever happened next, Maddie knew she had taken the first step by opening herself up to new possibilities. Maddie tucked a strand of her long, curly brown hair behind her ear as she strolled down Main Street, taking in the sights and sounds of the quaint small town. She breathed in the aroma of freshly baked bread wafting from the corner bakery and listened to the strumming guitar of a street musician perched on a nearby bench.

Though Maddie felt comforted by the quaintness of Mellow Creek, there was an underlying melancholy that clung to her like a shadow ever since losing Makenna. Everywhere she went held memories of her twin sister, of times they had explored the town with Grandma Minnie before. Passing the movie theater made her think of the comedies they used to sneak into on weekends. The local diner brought back images of late-night milkshake runs after baseball games. Even walking down Main Street reminded Maddie of leisurely window-shopping trips with Makenna, giggling over silly souvenirs and kitschy trinkets.

Maddie's reminiscing was interrupted by a tall figure emerging from the coffee shop up ahead, cradling a steaming cup in his hands. She recognized his messy blonde hair and plaid shirt immediately — it was Tristen again! Maddie's heart leapt at the serendipitous encounter.

As Tristen approached, Maddie tried to act casual, twirling a lock of hair around her finger. "Tristen…"

"Was this too soon?" Tristen asked as he handed her a

cup of coffee.

"Not at all," Maddie replied, hoping her nervousness didn't show.

"Triple mocha latte?" Tristen handed her a coffee.

"How did you?" Maddie was shocked that he knew her order.

"I have a good memory." Tristen tapped his finger on his head.

Maddie and Tristen were sitting on a bench, staring at the Mellow Creek all afternoon as people just went about their merry ways. Maddie was the first to speak. "So, it looks like summer's just getting started, huh?"

Tristen looked over at her and smiled. He hadn't expected her to be so forthright. "Yeah, I guess so. Same as usual, really."

"It must be nice to be just a normal summer day. I haven't felt normal for a while. Not since..." Maddie looked off in the distance, refusing to fill in the blanks.

"Makenna died?" supplied Tristen.

"How did you..." Maddie looked at him and tried to discern the truth.

"It was in the papers. Maddie, I'm sorry. I can't even imagine. She was such a wonderful person. I remember playing hide and seek until the fireflies stopped flashing."

"Even though you never told your father where you were?" asked Makenna with a faint smile.

"If he wanted to know, he should have paid attention." Tristen shrugged his shoulders with a wry grin.

They sat in silence for a few moments, as if the two teens were searching for a safe topic that wouldn't make either one of them feel like they were swimming in a pool of awkwardness. Maddie spoke again. "So, what about you? What have you been up to this summer?"

Tristen looked down at the ground, kicking a pebble

with the toe of his shoe. "I've been doing football training for my high school team," he said. "It's been really good so far."

Maddie nodded. "So he won?"

"Yeah, I guess he did." Tristen glanced up at Maddie, a hint of surprise in his eyes. "You remembered."

"How much you hated football?" Maddie put a hand on his lap. "We're all just living up to their expectations, aren't we?"

"I suppose we are. Let them win the small ones, so we can win the wars later, though, right?"

Maddie smiled. "Yeah, I guess. Some days, the fighting is too much, though, you know."

"I *do* know." Tristen's eyes met hers, and it was as if their two minds were one.

"You do..." Maddie whispered. Maddie had only ever felt that kind of mental connection with one other person in her life.

"You want to take a walk?" asked Tristen.

"Sure," agreed Maddie.

As they strolled down Main Street together, Maddie felt a glimmer of happiness amidst her grief. Though she still missed her sister deeply, being with Tristen gave her hope that she could open her heart again. She had a feeling this was just the beginning of an unforgettable summer.

"I should get going. My grandma's expecting me home soon," Maddie said reluctantly as their walk came to an end.

"Want a ride?" offered Tristen.

"No, I think I'd like to walk if you don't mind. It's a good day for it." Maddie had a lot to think about, and she wanted to be alone when she did.

"I'll text you," promised Tristen.

She nodded to him. "You better."

As she walked home alone, she glanced over her shoulder more than once, hoping to catch one last glimpse of Tristen. She couldn't remember the last time she felt this giddy. For the first time in months, she was excited about what the future might hold.

When she arrived home, her grandma looked up from the stove where she was cooking dinner. "You look happy," she remarked. "Have a nice walk?"

"The best," Maddie replied dreamily.

Grandma Minnie smiled knowingly, recognizing the look in her eyes. As they sat down to eat, Maddie found herself replaying every moment with Tristen, anticipation building inside her. She couldn't wait to see where her connection to Tristen might lead. Budding romance? Friend zone? Either way, Maddie would take what she could get.

Chapter 7

Grandma Minnie grabbed her sunhat and gardening gloves as she headed out the back door of the house. A warm breeze filtered through the leaves of the trees as Maddie trailed behind, her face concealed by a floppy hat and a pair of sunglasses. Grandma Minnie pointed out the occasional flower along the path, her voice calm and reassuring as she and Maddie walked toward the vegetable garden.

The sun glinted off the dew-laden blades of grass as they made their way down the walkway. Grandma Minnie inhaled the sweet scent of freshly cut hay and smiled as she glanced around the garden. The vegetable garden was a special place, a place where she and Maddie could spend time together in the warmth of the sun, in the solace of nature.

Maddie felt as though she were wrapped in a cocoon of safety and comfort with Grandma Minnie at their garden spot that day; it was something Maddie had never expected to feel from something so mundane. The birds chirped merrily from nearby branches while butterflies fluttered among the cascade of bright colors in their midst. They were starting their garden work in the flower beds this morning. Pink roses, yellow daisies – even random weeds couldn't take away from this slice of paradise today. Maddie refused to let this beautiful nature be ruined by anything, even the inner turmoil that was barely under the surface.

Grandma Minnie removed an old shovel plucked from one pocket and then another small trowel tucked into yet another pocket – they shared simplistic tools, but sometimes those simple utilitarian items provided just enough to enable them both to get lost in something productive that took just a bit of the sadness away from their lives. Gardening side by side gave life purpose again beyond grief or worry: connecting soil with seed reminded each what beauty can arise out of times that seem daunting and difficult. Resilient roots drew strength deep down and nourished new beginnings above ground through seasonal cycles. Life was a constant cycle. Happiness, sorrow, pain, strife, courage, hope. It had many seasons and could blossom even when there were obstacles ahead.

Working together in silence did more healing than talking ever could. This sweet silence gave them both time to heal in the ebb and flow of the gentle music between their hearts. It was everything that Maddie needed in those moments. And the fact that something else would grow from it made it all that much sweeter. Soon, they would find themselves lifting up fresh produce. Maddie appreciated the taste of homegrown garden vegetables much more than the over-chemicalized store ones any day of the week.

As Maddie dug at the ground, a small rock upturned, and a wave of emotions rippled through her. She remembered this rock. Makenna had painted it when she was just five. A small red ladybug with big, googly white eyes was lying on the ground in front of her. All at once, her mind was swarming with memories of the two of them in the garden together, chasing the beautiful butterflies as if they were magical fairies. The two of them twirled in handmade tutus and butterfly wings they had sprinkled with silver glitter to make themselves fly like Tinker Bell.

Grandma Minnie paused for a moment and turned to

Maddie, her brow furrowed with concern. She reached out and touched Maddie's arm, her voice gentle as she asked, "Are you okay, sweetheart?"

Maddie glanced up at her grandmother, her eyes glistening with unshed tears. Picking up the rock, she held it up mutely, and Grandma Minnie pulled her close, wrapping her arms around her in a comforting embrace.

"I miss her too, Maddie."

After a few moments, Grandma Minnie released Maddie and stood up. She smiled and held out her hand, and Maddie took it, allowing her grandmother to lead her to the vegetable garden. Grandma Minnie selected a basket and filled it with even more gardening tools. "Let's tend to some of these weeds, shall we?"

Grandma Minnie showed Maddie how to pull weeds, how to thin seedlings, and how to properly water the plants. With each lesson, Maddie's confidence grew, and her smile widened. Grandma Minnie watched with pride as Maddie confidently tackled each task, and Maddie felt a surge of pleasure as she saw the pride on her grandmother's face.

When the sun began to set, Grandma Minnie and Maddie returned to the house, their arms laden with freshly harvested vegetables. Grandma Minnie cooked them up into a delicious dinner, and Maddie watched in awe as her grandmother moved around the kitchen with the ease of a seasoned chef. After dinner, Grandma Minnie sat down with Maddie and told her stories of her childhood, of hunting for wildflowers with her own grandmother, of playing tag in the meadow, of picnicking at the river.

As Maddie listened to the stories, her love for her grandmother grew. By the time Grandma Minnie finished speaking, there was a spark of life in Maddie's eyes that hadn't been there before. The stories had given her a new lease on life, and for the first time in a long time, Maddie allowed herself to believe that everything would be okay.

Grandma Minnie and Maddie continued to spend time in the garden together for the next few days, and it wasn't long before the fruits of their labor began to show. As the summer sun shone down, the vegetables in the garden flourished, and Maddie's spirits lifted. She began to look forward to the times she spent in the garden, and soon, the thought of it brought a smile to her face.

This morning, there was not much need for gardening. They had done a fine job keeping it up. All that was required was a daily watering, which Maddie took care of the moment she got up. When she returned inside, she found Grandma Minnie doing laundry.

Grandma Minnie looked up from folding clothes, "Why don't you take a break today? Some of the teens spend time in town. You might make a few friends."

Maddie shifted nervously before taking a deep breath. "Maybe I could go to the library or something."

Grandma nodded slowly before giving Maddie an affectionate smile; "Very well," she said warmly. "But why don't you treat yourself to some lunch and maybe ice cream. You've been an awful good help here. My treat."

"You sure you don't want to go with me?" asked Maddie.

"No, you go get some freedom. Just don't get into too much trouble, or your dad will never let me hear the end of it." Grandma Minnie's grin set a sparkle to her eyes.

"Thanks, Grandma." Maddie hopped over to her and kissed her on the cheek. Maddie was excited to get a moment away. Maybe if she was lucky, she'd run into Tristen again. They had texted a few times, but he had been really busy with football. That or he was brushing her off.

Maddie did not give her grandma a chance to second-guess her decision. She grabbed her purse and took the money her grandma handed her, then headed straight for the door. Waving goodbye, she stepped out of the house feeling determined to have a small adventure.

Maddie explored the town. She walked past a flower shop bursting with color and couldn't resist going inside. The owner greeted her with a warm smile, and Maddie dove right into conversation with her. The woman showed her different arrangements and taught her the meanings of each flower. Maddie had a feeling her mother would fit right in at this flower shop if this were the one she was applying for a job.

Maddie browsed the bookstore next door, running her fingers over the spines of novels. She ended up buying a classic romance novel and then headed to the park to read it in peace. She passed groups of teenagers hanging out at the skate park or playing basketball, but she felt content just to sit on a bench, book in hand, and lose herself in the story.

As she read, Maddie's thoughts drifted back to Tristen. She wondered what he was doing at that moment. Was he thinking about her, too? Or had he completely forgotten about her? Maddie pushed those thoughts aside and focused on the book.

Eventually, hunger pangs drove Maddie to seek out food. She followed the scent of hot, fresh food, and it led her straight to the small-town diner, Ollie's. The diner was cozy and intimate, exactly what Maddie was looking for. She sat at the counter and perused the menu, finally settling on a milkshake and a burger. As she waited for her food, she began to people-watch. There were families chatting happily over plates of pancakes and eggs, gossiping old ladies sipping coffee, and young couples laughing together.

Suddenly, she spotted Tristen across the diner. He was sitting with a group of friends, laughing and joking around. Maddie's heart skipped a beat as he caught her eye and gave her a small wave. She waved back hesitantly, a blush creeping up her neck. Part of her wished he would invite her over, but it was clear that his group was a little too cramped for her tastes. Were they all football players and cheerleaders? Did that mean his image was the most important thing? Not that there was anything wrong with that crowd, it's just not the kind that ever accepted her before, and she didn't expect this town to be any different.

Her food came moments later, and Maddie tried to focus on her meal. But every time she looked up from her burger, her eyes were drawn back to Tristen. When he stood up from his table and started walking towards her, Maddie felt her nerves kick into overdrive. Great. What should she say to him? Accuse him of ghosting her? Starting with an attack wasn't exactly the right way to start a conversation.

"Hey," Tristen said with a grin as he took the seat next to hers.

"Hi," Maddie replied, feeling shy all of a sudden.

"I'm sorry I haven't been able to hang out much lately," Tristen said apologetically. "Football practice has been crazy."

"It's fine," Maddie replied with a small smile. She was actually relieved her assumption had been right. Otherwise, other nasty ones would start to rear their ugly head in her brain. Was he with Tiffany, and he just didn't want to tell her?

There was a brief pause before Tristen spoke up again. "Do you want to come hang out with me tonight? We're having a bonfire at the pond again."

Maddie's heart leapt at the invitation. "I'd love to."

"Great!" Tristen said with enthusiasm. "I'll text you the details."

Maddie watched as Tristen walked away, feeling a newfound excitement bubble up within her. She had never been to a bonfire before, and the thought of spending time with Tristen made her feel giddy. So he was comfortable introducing her to his friends. It felt like a half-hearted triumph. On one hand, he was bringing her into his world. On the other, she had to remind herself that they were nothing more than friends. It was her stupid brain that wanted to toss them together like a romantic teenage salad slathered in sweet, dream-filled Catalina dressing. Maddie was a blithering mess where he was concerned, all because the boy next door had turned into a young Chris Hemsworth lookalike.

As Maddie finished her meal, she couldn't help but daydream about what the night might bring. She imagined sitting close to Tristen, feeling the warmth of the fire against her skin as they talked and laughed together. Maybe he would even kiss her under the stars. Bring an imaginary hammer and whisk her somewhere into the heavens, away from this mortal world? Her very own Thor here to make her life better, one villain battle at a time? She really did need to find another hobby besides cataloging the heroic qualities of Marvel Avengers.

Maddie shook herself out of her reverie and paid for her meal. She was already in full plan mode. What would she wear? Shorts, shirt? Or did she dress up a little? What did one wear to a bonfire anyway? Maddie had never been to one before. She could only guess, really. By the end of the day, she'd probably tear her closet apart, finding the perfect outfit. If Makenna had been here, she'd have torn hers apart, too.

And commence stomach drop. How many minutes was it this time? How long had she gone without that feeling in the pit of her stomach? Maybe twenty this time. That was almost a new record, a small progress that felt limiting and heartbreaking at the same time. She didn't want every inch of her day filled with Makenna, but she didn't want to erase her either. There was this balance of when to let go and when to hold tight to all the things that made her feel closer to her sister. If only the main ties to her right now weren't the horrible pain that anchored her to the ground. She had to remind herself that everything was one day at a time, one breath at a time, one step at a time. Focus on the moment. That's what she had to do.

A fresh wind blew against her face as she exited the diner. The sweet smell of waffle cones wafted on the wind, and she was tempted to stop in for a cone to soothe her feelings away. Ice cream almost always made her feel better, but she was already stuffed from her late lunch. Besides, it was time to get back home so she could plan for the night. Who knew how many opportunities she would get like this? She was going to make the most of it while she could.

Chapter 8

Tristen arrived promptly at 7 p.m. to pick her up. Maddie saw him waiting outside and felt her heart skip a beat as she walked over to him. He looked handsome in a simple t-shirt and jeans, with his hair styled perfectly. She started to wonder if her shorts and summer blouse were going to be trendy enough to match his style, but it was too late to go back and change now. Besides, she really had torn through her wardrobe. There were now piles of clothes on the floor in small heaps. Maddie was not looking forward to putting it all away later, but that was tomorrow's problem. Tonight, she was going to focus on having a good time for once.

"Hey," he said with a smile as he took in her appearance.

"Hi," Maddie replied, feeling a blush creep up her cheeks.

Tristen grinned. "You look great."

Maddie felt flustered at his words. "Thank you."

"Of course. You ready to go?" Tristen looked through the door as if looking for some approval.

"Yep. Let me just tell Grandma Minnie we're leaving." Maddie walked into the kitchen where her grandma was sitting drinking her tea. "Gran, I'm heading out now."

"Okay, Maddie. Not too late. You know your curfew." Minnie reminded her.

"Yes, Ma'am," Maddie replied as she reached down to

kiss her grandma on the forehead. "I love you."

"Love you too, Maddie girl." Grandma Minnie leaned into her kiss and smiled.

Maddie walked back out to the front door and smiled at Tristen. "All good to go."

"This way, my lady," Tristen did an elaborate bow and twisted his hand in front of him to gesture toward his pickup truck. "Your chariot awaits."

"It's quite the chariot," teased Maddie.

"Trust me, I know. When your father owns three car lots and still gives you hand-me-downs from twenty years ago, it kinda chafes. No son of mine will be entitled…"

"At least you have wheels," pointed out Maddie

"True that." Tristen grinned. "They get me places."

"And into trouble, I bet," teased Maddie.

"I'll have you know I've been the model citizen." Tristen opened her door for her.

"I'm sure." Maddie got into the truck and got situated. "So, how far is this bonfire?"

"It's just up the road."

"Why didn't we just walk?" asked Maddie.

Tristen patted the steering wheel. "Mobile seating."

"Tailgating then?" Maddie didn't like the idea of some large football party out in the woods. Maybe this was a bad idea. She was sure to stick out like a sore thumb.

"Don't worry. We're not into wild parties. Small towns aren't always like the movies make them out to be. Just some friends hanging out. We may crank the music loud, but we're harmless."

The bonfire was located by a small pond on the outskirts of town, and when they arrived, they saw that there were already plenty of people gathered around the fire. Maddie recognized some of them from around town and church and others she didn't know. Most of them seemed nice enough on the surface, but there was a layer of tension that Maddie wasn't sure how to get through. The only one who was throwing her shade really was Tiffany, but at least for now, the cheerleader kept her thoughts to herself. Somehow, though, Maddie didn't think it would last. It was clear that Tiffany wasn't happy that Tristen had brought her along. Maddie wasn't sure if Tristen had been clear enough with Tiffany in the past. Bringing Maddie along sent a message that maybe words could not translate. Maddie wasn't very happy about being in the middle of it all, but there was a little satisfaction seeing her seething just a bit. Maybe Maddie did have a tiny bone in her body that wanted to see her squirm just a little, especially with as haughty as she had treated her the first night she had met her.

Tristen must have sensed her discomfort because he put his arm protectively around her and gave her a squeeze. She smiled at him, grateful for his presence. He was the only one who truly made her feel like she belonged in this small town.

"So, what do you guys usually do out here?" Maddie asked Tristen, hoping to break the ice with everyone else.

Tristen grinned and looked around the fire. "Oh, we talk about whatever is on our minds: school stuff, current events, music…whatever it may be. We also play some games like truth or dare or two truths and a lie. It's all just for fun, though; nothing serious." He paused and looked around again before continuing: "Sometimes we even take out the guitars and drums that people bring for some impromptu jam sessions. Everybody loves it when that happens."

Maddie smiled as she watched everyone relaxing around the bonfire, laughing and talking amongst themselves like they'd known each other their whole lives. She could feel herself starting to relax, too; maybe this wasn't going to be so bad after all.

As the night went on, they roasted marshmallows over the fire, drank soda, and played music on a portable speaker. Maddie felt happy to be included in their group and even managed to strike up a conversation with Tristen's best friend, Tyler.

As they laughed and talked, Maddie couldn't help but notice the way Tristen kept stealing glances at her. She felt a warmth in her chest, knowing that he was interested in her too. Something small was starting to grow here, and while she was in unknown territory, Maddie was excited to find out where it might all go.

The sun had set, and the stars were starting to twinkle in the sky when Tristen took Maddie's hand and led her away from the group. "Let's go for a walk."

Maddie felt a flutter in her stomach as they walked hand-in-hand along the water's edge. The moon cast a soft glow over everything, making it feel like they were in their own little world. She could almost block out the sounds of the bonfire from behind them.

They walked for a while in comfortable silence before Tristen finally spoke up. "I'm really glad you came tonight, Maddie."

"I'm glad, too," she replied softly.

"I know I've been distant lately with football and all, but I want you to know that I haven't forgotten about you," Tristen said earnestly.

"I haven't forgotten about you either," she admitted. If she told him how often he took up space in her mind, he would probably start running for the hills. She felt slightly obsessed.

Tristen stopped walking and turned to face her. "Maddie, I like you. A lot."

Maddie's heart skipped a beat as she realized what he was saying. She had been hoping for this moment since she arrived in town. "I like you too, Tristen."

Tristen took a step closer and leaned down, pressing his lips to hers. It was a simple kiss, the first of its kind in Maddie's universe, lasting just long enough to leave a warm impression on her lips. She closed her eyes to take in all of it. The sounds of music pumping in the background, the breeze on her face, the way her cheeks warmed up at the thought of kissing him again, all of it circled around inside her, planting roots in her memories for years to come.

When they broke the kiss, neither one of them said a word. Maddie wasn't even sure she had the words for what had just happened. She had never expected Tristen to kiss her tonight. Part of her was still trying to figure out if it had just happened. She wasn't even sure what this would mean for them. Did one kiss make them an item? Was there a social contract for something like that? Had anyone else witnessed it? They were pretty far from the bonfire right now, so chances of that were slim, but still…someone could have seen. And what if they had? Would they make a big deal and start busting his chops of something? Make a few digs about it? Maddie tried not to worry about that and held onto the quiet excitement that was bursting inside her.

They stood there for a few more minutes, just enjoying the peacefulness of the night and the feeling of being in each other's company. Maddie didn't want this moment to end. It was perfect in every way, not clouded with any other emotions other than the joy of new discovery. She longed to feel more moments just like it.

Eventually, Tristen spoke up. "Let's go back to the bonfire. Everyone is probably wondering where we went."

Maddie nodded, feeling a little disappointed that their private moment was coming to an end. But she was also excited to be with Tristen around people again, knowing that they now shared a special connection.

As they walked back to the fire, Maddie felt like she was walking on clouds. She was grateful for this little adventure and the unexpected turn it had taken. Maybe small-town life wasn't so bad after all. Life could be better here if she just gave it a chance. At least, that was where her brain had landed until she saw the one thing she never expected to see.

"Dad?" Maddie felt her joy melt away like a pat of butter sliding over a stack of burning pancakes when she saw her father searching the crowd of kids for her with a frantic, maniacal look on his face.

"Where have you been?" he asked sternly.

"We went for a walk," Tristen replied, his voice calm.

Maddie's father folded his arms across his chest. "It's getting late, Maddie. You're coming home."

Tristen nodded. "I was just taking her home now."

"I'm sure *you* were. And what are you all doing out here? I have half a mind to make a call to the sheriff's department." Robert Tyler looked at the teens and shook his head. "Half of you are probably on the football team too. When I start coaching, I'll put a stop to this. That's one thing you can count on."

The crowd went quiet, and the music shut off as Robert went on his tirade. Maddie looked down at the ground, wishing the dirt would swallow her whole. The night had been perfect for once, up until the point where her father had to come in and ruin it. With a feeling of dread, Maddie realized that her father had annihilated her chances of being accepted in this crowd. They were already making remarks behind their hands as they stared at her. Social outcast, party of one. At least she should be used to it by now. Being the sister of a dying cancer kid had pretty much paved the way for her social standing long ago. Why should Mellow Creek be any different?

"Dad?" Maddie moved to meet him, dread pooling in

her stomach. "Can you stop, please?"

Robert's eyes blazed as he took in the scene. "I'm taking you home. Now."

"But Dad —"

"Don't 'but Dad' me." He grabbed her arm. "I told you no parties."

Maddie wrenched her arm away, anger rising. "You're embarrassing me! I'm not a child."

"You're seventeen. Legally, you're still a child." Robert crossed his arms. "We're leaving. Your grandmother must be worried sick."

"Grandma Minnie told me I could go."

Tristen appeared at Maddie's side, bristling. "Mr. Tyler, we weren't doing anything wrong. There's no alcohol here."

Robert turned his glare on the boy. "Stay out of this. It's none of your business."

"Dad, stop!" Maddie wedged herself between them before things could escalate. She met Robert's stern gaze. "I'll go with you. Just...let me say goodbye."

Robert huffed. "Five minutes. I'll be waiting by the car."

As he marched off, Maddie turned to Tristen, humiliation burning through her. The party had gone silent, all eyes on the drama.

"I'm so sorry," she said. "I have to go."

Tristen gave her a sympathetic look. "It's okay. Overprotective dads, you know?" He squeezed her hand. "See you soon?"

Maddie managed a small smile. "Yeah. See you."

She hurried after Robert, his anger permeating the tense, silent drive back to Grandma Minnie's. Maddie leaned her head against the window, confused and frustrated. Why was he acting like this? She just wanted to feel normal again.

To feel anything but the gaping loss of her sister. And she had. Maddie had felt normal like life might exist outside the tragedy that had taken over her world.

"I don't want you seeing that boy again," he finally said, his voice hard.

Maddie turned to him in disbelief. "Why? Tristen is nice, he—"

"You don't know anything about him!" Her dad slammed his hand against the steering wheel. "I won't have you getting mixed up with the wrong crowd."

"The wrong crowd? Dad, they're just normal kids!"

He shook his head. "I saw the way those girls looked at you. Like you didn't belong." His face softened slightly. "Maddie, I just want to protect you."

"I don't need to be protected." Maddie crossed her arms, sinking lower in her seat. She thought of the thrill she'd felt at the party, the way Tristen made her feel seen. And how quickly it had all disappeared at the sight of her dad.

She turned her head to look out into the darkness as they drove over the bumpy back roads. Confusion and anger battled inside her. She just wanted to feel normal again, to have friends and a life of her own. But her dad seemed determined to keep her in the past, tethered to the grief that surrounded them like a fog.

Maddie sighed, the weight of loss settling over her once more. She rested her head against the window as they drove on through the night, the bright lights of the party fading to darkness behind them.

Later, Maddie lay in bed that night, thoughts churning. The pounding music and laughter from the pond party replayed in her mind, so different from the quiet clinking of silverware and murmur of conversation at the diner earlier that day. She had felt like a new person at the party — welcomed, included, alive. The cheerleaders' initial wary glances had melted into friendly smiles as Tristen introduced her around. Well, almost. Tiffany's smile had been fake, and Maddie had caught a few death glares a hand full of times. It was something she was prepared to deal with, though.

For the first time since Makenna got sick, Maddie didn't feel like "the girl with the dead sister." She was just Maddie, hanging out with new friends. Until Dad showed up, shattering the illusion. His anger and embarrassment flooded back to her in waves, leaving her disoriented. She thought of Tristen's easygoing confidence as he stood up to her father. A pang of longing caught her by surprise. Tristen saw her as she wanted to be seen — as her own person, not defined by her grief. The way he looked at her made her feel capable of anything, even moving on.

As she finally drifted off, Maddie resolved to push back against her father's smothering overprotection. If she didn't keep living, keep growing, Makenna's death would swallow her whole. She had to hold onto that glowing feeling from the party. She wouldn't let anyone's expectations trap her in the past.

Chapter 9

Maddie couldn't believe that her father had embarrassed her so much. How could he show up at the bonfire and make such a scene? How would she get through the rest of the summer without being a social pariah? She spent the next few days in her room, refusing to come out. Thankfully, her father had left already, leaving her to her peace once again.

As Maddie lay on her bed, staring at the ceiling, she couldn't help but feel trapped. Trapped by her father's actions, trapped by the expectations of her peers, and most of all, trapped by her own fears. She was so lost in her thoughts that she nearly missed the sound of her phone buzzing.

It was Tristen. Her heart skipped a beat as she read his message. "Can we talk?"

Maddie hesitated for a moment. She wasn't sure if she was ready to face him yet. Not to mention, her father had pretty much forbidden her from doing so, but he wasn't here now, was he? He had gone back to Maryland just as fast as he'd come. He'd only been here to check in with his new boss, fill out some paperwork or something like that. It had really been a fluke that Maddie had been caught really. Grandma Minnie had headed to the store, so she was home alone right now. What did she have to lose? She took a deep breath and replied, "Sure."

Within minutes, Tristen was standing outside the back

door. Maddie opened it and stepped outside without a word. The two walked to the bench near the garden and sat down before facing each other in silence.

"I'm sorry for how everything went down," he finally said.

"It's not your fault," Maddie replied quickly. "I don't blame you."

"I just don't want you to think I'm not here for you," Tristen said softly. "I should have texted you before now."

Maddie looked at him and felt a wave of emotion wash over her. With everything that had happened over the past few days, it was easy to forget how much she was starting to care for him.

"I know," she said, reaching out and taking his hand. "And thank you for being here now."

Their eyes met, and in that moment, Maddie knew she wanted nothing more than to be with Tristen. They leaned in closer until their lips almost touched, but Maddie was distracted by the butterfly that flitted here and there. It reminded her of her sister, and her mood plummeted. No sister, a father who didn't want her to live her life, and a budding love that might be torn away from her before it ever had a chance to blossom. It just wasn't fair. She pulled away. "I'm not sure we should be doing this."

"Did I do something wrong?" Tristen's face was filled with confusion, but Maddie couldn't answer him.

"If my dad knew..."

"You're probably right. I don't want you to do anything you're uncomfortable with or something that will get you into trouble, Maddie. I just...I feel different with you." Tristen looked down at his feet, his face downcast. "I was hoping for something real for a change."

"Me too," whispered Maddie. Her hand squeezed his. "But I need time to figure this out."

"Time." Tristen was disappointed with her words. He swallowed and shook his head. "Take what you need, Maddie. I'll be here when you're ready."

Maddie reached over and kissed him on the cheek. "Thank you, Tristen. I'll be in touch."

"I hope so." He smiled softly at her before standing up. Turning to walk away, he nodded to her one last time before he disappeared from sight.

As she lay in bed that night, Maddie couldn't help but feel guilty for letting Tristen down. But she knew she needed to take some time to deal with her emotions and sort out her feelings for him. How did she explain the guilt that wrapped around her heart? That she was alive and experiencing things that her sister would never get a chance to? Wouldn't that just push him away further? It was a piece he wasn't privy to, one that she was afraid to share. It was her decision what layers to peel back, and right now, she was standing firm to the one she presented to the outside world. Strong, solid, determined. Inside, she was anything but.

Maddie slept fitfully that night. The next day, she was determined to do something that would distract her. She spent the day helping in the garden before moving on to the attic. Grandma Minnie had several boxes she needed help going through as she tried to downsize her life. Maddie was finally on the boxes that had been saved in the closet of her room. These were momentos of the twins' childhood, projects they had worked on with Grandma Minnie each time they had come to stay. Maddie sifted through the cluttered boxes in her closet. Each item she touched was a painful reminder of what she had lost. Her fingers brushed against the frayed edges of an old painting depicting two smiling girls beneath a sprawling oak tree. She paused, pulling it from the box with trembling hands.

The faded acrylics flooded her mind with memories

— lazy summer days spent with Makenna beneath the shade of swaying branches. Mixing paints from the kits their dad had gifted them, giggling as they tried to capture the dappled sunlight on canvas. A sob caught in Maddie's throat as she traced her finger over the messy signature in the corner, right next to her own.

"I miss you so much, Kenna," Maddie whispered, hot tears spilling down her cheeks. She could almost hear her sister's voice in the rustle of wind through the trees outside her window. Feel the playful nudge of her elbow as they painted side by side.

Maddie clutched the canvas to her chest, overcome with grief. She longed to turn back the hands of time, to live once more in that moment of joy. But the stillness in the room was deafening, a reminder that she was now alone. Wiping her eyes, Maddie tucked the painting under her arm and headed outside, each step weighted by sorrow. She needed to feel close to Makenna again. Grabbing up her painting supplies, Makenna was determined to let her feelings flow freely where no one else could filter them.

As she stepped outside, the scent of freshly cut grass filled her nostrils, and she looked out to the sprawling yard where Makenna had spent hours playing and painting with her. Maddie felt a pang of longing in her chest as she remembered the sound of Makenna's laughter echoing through the yard. She walked past the swings, where they used to sit for hours, talking about everything and nothing at all. The painting felt heavy in her arms, a bittersweet reminder of happier times.

As she reached their tree, Maddie sank down onto the ground and leaned against its thick trunk. She closed her eyes and inhaled deeply, savoring the earthy scent of bark and leaves, imagining that Makenna was sitting beside her.

Maddie pulled the painting closer to her chest and

took a deep breath. She set it on the ground and picked up the blank canvas she had brought with her. It was time to let go of some of the grief and pain that had paralyzed her for so long. With trembling hands, she picked up a brush and started to paint. The colors flowed from her fingers onto the canvas like water pouring from a pitcher. She painted until she lost track of time until the sun began to dip beneath the horizon. Only then did the tears start to flow.

"Why did you have to leave me?" Maddie cried out, her voice breaking. "It's not fair!"

She could almost see Makenna sitting beside her, sunlight dappling her smiling face. Hear her sweet laugh ringing out like a melody. It was all she ever wanted.

"I'm so angry and confused," Maddie continued. "You were my best friend, my other half. How can I go on without you?"

The wind picked up, caressing her cheek like a gentle hand. Maddie closed her eyes, imagining her sister's embrace.

"I know you didn't want to go," she whispered. "But I feel so abandoned. Like there's this gaping hole inside me that nothing can fill."

Everything seemed too bright, too loud, too overwhelming. Her breath came faster, and she could feel her heart pounding in her chest. Her emotions were boiling over like a kettle ready to expel its top in one angry howl of oppression.

"It's not fair!" Maddie burst out suddenly. She swiped angrily at the tears that spilled down her cheeks. "Why did you have to leave me, Kenna? We were supposed to do everything together!"

She sank to her knees in the brittle grass, overcome. "You promised you wouldn't go where I couldn't follow. But you left me behind!"

Maddie pounded the ground with her fists. "It should

have been me, not you. You deserved to live so much more than I do."

Her shoulders shook with sobs as she rocked back and forth. "What am I supposed to do now? How can I go on without you?"

The wind carried the faint echo of laughter, two young voices raised in joy. Maddie's head jerked up, eyes searching even though she knew she would find nothing. The sound faded as quickly as it came.

"I'm so lost without you, Kenna," Maddie whispered. She wrapped her arms around herself. "I don't know if I can be me without you being you."

The grass rustled softly in response. Maddie let out a long, shaky breath. She stood up slowly, brushing the dirt from her knees. Maddie wiped her eyes, taking a deep, shuddering breath. The ache of loss still gripped her heart, but sitting here beneath their special tree, she could feel Makenna's presence. It gave her the faintest glimmer of peace.

Maddie let her fingers trail over the carved initials on the tree trunk. M + M Forever. She and Makenna had etched them there years ago, giggling as they promised to be best friends for life. Now Maddie was alone, the future stretching bleakly before her. She drew her knees to her chest, shoulders shaking with suppressed sobs.

"I don't know how to do this without you," she choked out. "Everything reminds me of you. Your empty bed, your clothes still hanging in the closet..."

She buried her face in her hands. "It's like you're a ghost haunting my every step. I both wish you were here and need you to be gone. I'm so confused..."

The wind whispered through the leaves once more. Maddie looked up, tears glistening on her cheeks.

"I know, I know," she said with a sad smile. "I have to keep living. For both of us now."

She let her fingers linger on the carved initials. "You'll always be a part of me, Kenna. My sister, my heart, my everything."

Maddie stood slowly, gazing up at the oak. Its solid presence reassured her. This tree had sheltered their childhood secrets, their dreams and fears. It would watch over her still.

"I'll come back soon," she promised softly. Then, shoulders back, she turned and walked away. One small step at a time into the future.

Maddie's steps slowed as she moved further from the oak tree. Maddie walked until the oak tree was out of sight, her footsteps heavy. She had no destination in mind, only a need to keep moving. To stop was to get lost in the swirling darkness inside her.

She came upon the park where she and Kenna used to play as children. The swings swayed empty in the breeze, chains creaking. Placing her painting supplies to the side, Maddie sank down onto one, wrapping her hands around the cold metal links.

"Remember how we used to see who could swing higher?" she asked softly. "You always won. I could never catch up no matter how hard I tried."

Maddie blinked back tears. "I wish you were here to beat me again."

The swing beside her moved slightly as if touched by an invisible hand. Maddie's breath caught.

"Kenna?" she whispered. "Is that you?"

The air seemed to shimmer where Kenna once sat. Maddie tentatively reached out a hand toward the apparition. Her fingers passed through empty space.

She exhaled, equal parts disappointment and hope. "I guess I'll never stop looking for you, will I?"

The silver moonlight filtered through the branches, casting shadows across Maddie's face as she sat hunched over on the swings. Maddie did not see or hear Tristen's approach. Tristen hesitated under the cover of darkness. "Maddie?" he called softly.

She flinched, shoulders tensing. Slowly, she raised her head, eyes widening at the sight of him.

"Tristen?" Her voice cracked. "What are you doing here?"

He moved closer, boots crunching over fallen leaves. "I saw you leave the tree."

She turned away, wiping her cheeks. "You shouldn't have followed me."

"I know." He sat down on the swing beside her. "But I couldn't leave you out here alone."

Silence stretched between them. Somewhere in the distance, an owl hooted. Tristen seemed to study her profile — the slope of her nose, the quiver of her lips. "You can talk to me, Maddie. Tell me anything."

"It's only been a few months," she whispered. "Since Makenna —"

Her breath hitched, fresh tears spilling down her cheeks. Before he could stop himself, Tristen slid his swing closer and wrapped an arm around her shoulders. She stiffened, then relaxed against him.

"I'm here," he murmured.

She buried her face in his shirt, muffling her sobs. He held her trembling frame. "I wish I could take away your pain."

"Me too," whispered Maddie through her tears.

The owl hooted again, a mournful sound. Maddie pulled away, wiping her eyes. She stood abruptly as if just realizing what time it was. "I should go. My grandma will wonder where I am."

Tristen rose, too. "Will you be okay?"

She managed a faint smile. "I'll be fine."

Maddie walked quickly down the street, random leaves and twigs crunching under her feet. The owl continued its lonely calls as she navigated by moonlight back to the dirt road. She could still feel the ghost of Tristen's arm around her, the steady beat of his heart. He had held her so gently as if she were made of glass. For that brief moment, she hadn't felt so alone.

But allowing herself to take comfort in him was dangerous. From what Grandma Minnie had told her, their families had been rivals ever since her dad played football in high school. The two had constantly been vying for the spotlight. Her father would be furious if he knew Tristen had followed her or that the two of them were forming any kind of relationship.

She reached the end of the dirt road, the lights of her house flickering in the distance. Grandma Minnie's used to feel warm and full of laughter. Now, it was suffocating in its emptiness. Her twin was gone, leaving a Maddie-shaped hole in her wake.

As she slipped through the back door and crept up to her room, Maddie made a decision. She would talk to Tristen again, no matter what their families thought. For the first time since Makenna got sick, she felt a glimmer of hope in the darkness. Maybe with Tristen by her side, she could begin to heal.

Later, Maddie lay in bed, staring up at the glow-in-the-dark stars still stuck to the ceiling from when she and Makenna were kids. They used to stay up late at night making up constellations, giggling under the covers with flashlights. Now, Maddie slept in this room alone. She could still see the faint outline where Makenna's bed used to be before her father moved it to the garage. Out of sight, but the emptiness still remained.

Maddie replayed the moment with Tristen over and

over. The way he had brushed the hair back from her face so gently, his eyes searching hers in the moonlight. She had thought, just for a second, that he might kiss her again. And despite herself, she had wanted him to.

But then that stupid owl. Its call had startled them apart, and the moment shattered. Maddie flushed with embarrassment, remembering how she had mumbled an excuse and hurried off, leaving Tristen standing there looking confused.

She wished she had handled it better. The way he had comforted her, she knew he cared. And she was starting to realize that she cared too, in a way she never expected.

Tomorrow, Maddie decided. Tomorrow, she would find Tristen and try again.

Maddie rolled over, punching her pillow in frustration. She wanted to talk to Tristen again, but doubt crept in. What if he regretted last night? Maybe he had just felt sorry for her in the moment. What if her baggage was too much for him to carry? There were plenty of other girls around, ready to slide into his life. None of them probably had dead sister drama to deal with.

The glow-in-the-dark stars on the ceiling seemed to taunt her. Makenna would tell her to go for it, to take a chance. But Makenna wasn't here anymore to give advice. She was alone.

Maddie sighed, memories of her sister flooding back. The laughter they had shared in this room, secrets whispered late into the night. How Makenna had held her hand in the hospital, reassuring her even as the cancer wasted her body away. Telling Maddie to live life to the fullest when she was gone.

A tear slipped down Maddie's cheek. She roughly brushed it away. Crying wouldn't bring Makenna back. And her sister was right — she had to start taking chances. That was the only way to break this vicious, lonely cycle.

Chapter 10

The garden exploded with color. Bright red tulips swayed gently in the breeze while vibrant yellow daffodils dotted the grass like splashes of sunshine. Grandma Minnie's prize roses climbed the wooden trellis in hues of pink, orange and white, filling the air with their sweet perfume.

Maddie sat cross-legged on the stone pathway that wound through the garden, absentmindedly picking at a loose thread on her faded jeans. Her dark hair fell in messy waves around her shoulders, and her eyes were distant, still puffy and red from crying earlier that morning. Maddie had dreamed about Makenna again and woke up feeling frozen and raw.

Grandma Minnie settled slowly onto the bench beside her, the wood creaking slightly under her weight. Though her movements were slower these days, her eyes remained as lively and kind as ever. She took Maddie's hand in her wrinkled one and gave it a gentle squeeze.

"Your sister loved this garden," she said softly. "She could spend hours out here, naming all the flowers and chasing butterflies."

Maddie nodded, blinking back fresh tears. "I miss her so much, Grandma," she whispered. "Everything reminds me of her."

Grandma Minnie pulled Maddie close, stroking her

hair. "I know, dear. But she'll always be with you, in your heart and your memories."

They sat in silence for a while, watching a pair of hummingbirds dart from flower to flower. The clouds drifted across the sky, filtering the sunlight into dappled patches on the ground. A slow peace started to settle.

"It's hard, but the pain will get easier over time," Grandma said gently. "You have to keep living your life. It's what Makenna would have wanted."

Maddie knew Grandma Minnie was right. As much as it hurt, she had to keep going for her sister's sake. She took a deep breath of the sweet floral air. "Will you help me plant some forget-me-nots for her next spring?"

Grandma Minnie smiled. "Of course, sweetheart. We'll plant a whole garden in her memory."

Grandma Minnie gently took Maddie's hand in her wrinkled one, giving it a gentle squeeze. "I know it's hard, but you have to keep living. Your sister wouldn't want you to stop enjoying life."

Maddie nodded, blinking back tears. "I'll try, Gran. It's just...everything reminds me of her."

"I understand, dear." Grandma Minnie paused, looking thoughtful. "You know, your father went through rough times when he was younger. too."

Maddie looked up, surprised. Her dad rarely talked about his childhood. He was often the strong, silent type, so wound up running their lives that he sometimes forgot to give himself a moment to break. She had only seen him break once, and Maddie would never forget it. That was the moment Makenna's casket lowered to the ground. Maddie hadn't been prepared for the sobs that had left his chest, like a wounded bear caught in a trap. Maddie never wanted to hear him cry like that ever again.

"Back when your father was in high school, he was the

only black player on his football team," Grandma explained. "It was a different time then — this was the late 80s in a small southern town. As you can imagine, he faced a lot of racism from his teammates and coaches. One boy in particular, Daniel Grant, was especially cruel to your father. He would taunt him with racial slurs and trip him during plays. Just petty, mean-spirited things." Grandma Minnie shook her head.

"That must have been so hard for Dad," Maddie said softly. It was a different world now, but Maddie had enough experiences herself to understand how her father must have felt.

"It was. But your father never retaliated. He kept turning the other cheek, staying focused on the game. Until one day, Daniel took things too far."

Grandma Minnie described the horrific incident when her father had become injured during practice in a botched play that Daniel had orchestrated. Her father had been sidelined for weeks. The racial abuse had finally become physical harm.

"Your father had every right to be angry," Grandma said. "He never retaliated, but he never forgave him either. Although that fool Grant seemed to think your dad had something to do with him getting benched at the playoff game. Those two are like oil and gasoline."

Maddie shifted uncomfortably on the stone bench, avoiding her grandmother's gaze. She knew exactly where this story was headed. "Dad doesn't want me seeing Tristen anymore. He says Tristen's a bad influence."

Grandma Minnie nodded knowingly. "Let me guess — Tristen's the boy from the bonfire?"

Maddie smiled slightly. "Yeah, that's him. Dad thinks he's dangerous. But he's not! He's really sweet, and he understands me in a way other people don't."

"Is that right?" asked Grandma Minnie.

"Gran, he's the only one I've talked to about Makenna. It's like he gets it because he knew her, too. He listens without tuning me out like the rest of my friends did."

"That's a gift," agreed Minnie.

"I just feel so connected to him, like he's the only one who really gets me," Maddie concluded, her eyes glistening with tears.

Grandma Minnie reached over and squeezed her hand. "Oh, sweetie, I know it's hard. Your daddy just wants to protect you — but he needs to understand that people aren't always what they seem."

She tilted Maddie's chin up gently. "Maybe he will come around."

"I doubt it. Besides, Dad's not even here to talk to."

Grandma Minnie gave Maddie a sympathetic smile. "I know, dear. But don't give up hope just yet. You never know what might happen."

With that, the two of them sat in comfortable silence, watching as the sun slowly started to set over the garden. Maddie couldn't help but feel grateful for her grandmother's presence and support during this difficult time in her life.

As they got up to leave, Maddie couldn't help but think about Tristen. Despite her father's disapproval, she knew deep down that she couldn't give him up so easily. She had to find a way to convince her dad that Tristen was a good person, that he wasn't dangerous like he thought.

But how? Maddie wondered as she walked back towards the house with Grandma Minnie. How could she prove to her father that Tristen was worthy of her love?

As if on cue, her phone buzzed in her pocket, interrupting her thoughts. It was a message from Tristen: "Hey beautiful, thinking about you. Want to meet up later?"

Maddie smiled to herself. Maybe this was the perfect opportunity to show her father that Tristen wasn't who he thought he was. She quickly typed out a response: "Yes, I'll meet you at the park in an hour."

As she hit send, Maddie felt a sense of determination wash over her. She was going to show her father that Tristen was worth fighting for, no matter what it took.

"Do you mind if I meet a friend in town?" asked Maddie.

"If by friend you mean Tristen, I know nothing of the sort." Grandma Minnie winked at her. "Just don't do anything crazy. I trust you have a good head on your shoulders?"

"We'll just go see a movie or something," Maddie said, trying to hide her nerves. "I promise I'll be safe."

"Alright, alright," Grandma Minnie said, chuckling. "Just be back by curfew."

Maddie felt a surge of gratitude towards her grandmother. She knew that not all parents or grandparents would be as understanding as she was. Grandma Minnie was a jewel, something Maddie would never forget, and that made her want to make sure to be home well within her curfew limits to avoid causing any more trouble for her grandmother.

As she walked towards the park, Maddie's mind buzzed with thoughts of Tristen. He was waiting for her under a big oak tree with his arms open wide.

"Hey," he said, giving her a warm hug. "I've missed you."

"I've missed you too," Maddie replied, resting her head on his chest. She felt so safe in his arms, like nothing could hurt her.

Tristen pulled back and looked into her eyes. "What's wrong? You seem tense."

"It's my dad," Maddie said, biting her lip nervously. "My Gran told me about our family's history."

"What history?"

"Our fathers hate each other," Maddie tried to explain.

"Some football drama from way back when."

Maddie did not want to go into too many details. How did she tell someone that his father was a closeted racist? Maybe he wasn't closeted, though. Maybe Daniel Grant still hated people based on the color of their skin. Maddie did have obvious feelings about that, but she wasn't romantically involved with him. She was involved with Tristen, and as far as she could tell, he had no problem with the color of her skin.

"Why does it always come back to football?" Tristen ran his fingers through his hair. "Everywhere I turn!"

"I know," Maddie said, reaching for his hand. "But I don't care what either one of them thinks. I believe in us."

Tristen gave her hand a reassuring squeeze. "Then we'll fight for us together."

Tristen leaned in and kissed her softly, and Maddie melted into his embrace. In that moment, she knew that she would do whatever it took to convince her father that Tristen was worth fighting for. And with that thought in mind, Maddie knew that she would never give up on their love, no matter how hard the road ahead might be. She was determined to fight for them, to prove to her father that Tristen was the real deal, and most importantly, to honor Makenna's memory by living life to the fullest.

Chapter 11

Time had a way of passing faster than Maddie really wanted it to. The summer was almost up, and now her parents were moving back to Mellow Creek. They had found a new house for them to live in, which meant that it was time to move out of Grandma Minnie's. They were just moving across town, though, so at least she could see Grandma Minnie anytime she wanted to. The two of them had become thick as thieves over the summer.

Today, Maddie was helping her parents at the new house, well new to them. Like most of the houses in Mellow Creek, it had already been passed down one generation or another. Even so, it was a new start for her family. Maddie stepped out of the moving truck, shielding her eyes from the glaring sun. The old Victorian house loomed in front of her, the peeling paint and creaking porch contrasting sharply with the sleek modern houses that lined the rest of the street.

"Well, here we are," said Robert, hauling a box up the front steps. "Home sweet home."

Maddie eyed the crooked shutters critically. They looked like they had seen better days. She already missed her old room, with its lilac walls that she and Makenna had painted themselves. Here, Makenna left no trace. She had never lived within these walls, so her life and memory would never project anywhere in its walls. Maddie would still try to find ways to seek her out in her own little way, no matter how much everyone seemed to want her to disappear.

Her mother, Jamie, emerged from the house, wiping sweat from her brow. "Oh good, you're here," she said. "The movers already brought in the big furniture, but there are still plenty of boxes."

As Maddie dragged her suitcase up the steps, she thought longingly in the direction of Grandma Minnie's house across town. What she wouldn't give to be sitting on Gran's front porch sipping some ice tea with her right now. Or even weeding with her in the garden. Maddie had gotten used to their pattern. It was easy to get into a groove and ease into her days with Grandma Minnie. Maddie always knew what to expect.

Robert seemed to sense Maddie's hesitation. "I know it's not what you're used to," he said gently. "But Grandma Minnie is just down the block. We'll make this place feel like home in no time."

Maddie nodded, swallowing the lump in her throat. She knew her parents were doing their best — her dad's job at the insurance agency was starting this week, and it was flexible enough to allow for his coaching hours at the high school. Her mom was going to be working at a local flower shop. Both of them had their lives all sorted. And Maddie, she was expected to attend the new high school like nothing ever happened. She wasn't looking forward to it, not really. Maddie didn't hate the idea of school. It was the starting over as the awkward new girl who had to pretend to be something she wasn't just so people would like her. That social game was exhausting, and Maddie had already learned there were far more important things in life, like surviving, for one.

Still, as Maddie stepped across the threshold of this old house, it was hard not to wish for the life she'd left behind. She vowed to turn her new room into a bright, happy space

— a blank canvas full of potential. For now, that possibility was enough to lift her spirits.

Maddie wandered through the empty first floor, peeking into what would become the living room and kitchen. She could envision where they would place the furniture and hang family photos on the walls. It would turn into a comfortable space. She was sure of that. Like her, it just needed a little time to settle.

As she climbed the creaking steps to the second floor, she thought of Tristen. How was she going to continue seeing him behind her father's back? Sooner or later, her dad would figure it out, especially since he was going to be coaching the football team. She hadn't thought this out very well yet. Grandma Minnie had made it easy for them to see each other, trusting Maddie to make responsible decisions. She probably did so because she felt sorry for Maddie. Part of Maddie knew she had taken advantage of that, but she tried not to feel too bad about it. For once, she had started to feel like a normal teenage girl with hopes and dreams that hadn't been crushed under the weight of despair.

Maddie pushed open the door to her new bedroom. Pale rectangles on the wall showed where previous occupants had hung posters and pictures. The late afternoon sun streamed through the large window, making the hardwood floors glow. She set her suitcase on the bed and began unpacking clothes into the antique dresser. Lining up her books on the shelves, she arranged photos of her friends on the desk. When she was done, the room still felt sterile and unfamiliar. Maddie sighed.

She wished she could throw up a few photos of her and Tristen there to help her make it feel like home. That would definitely not fly, though. Her dad would definitely lose his mind if he saw proof that Maddie was defying his rules. She wasn't in any hurry for him to find out about it either.

Maddie stared at the blank walls, imagining how she

could make this space her own. Then she remembered — her dad had given her permission to paint anything she wanted, even if she wanted to paint murals. She could cover the walls with scenes from her favorite books, lyrics from songs she and Tristen listened to, and inside jokes only the two of them understood. The possibilities swirled in her mind.

Maddie dug through the moving boxes until she found her art supplies. She set up a palette of acrylic paints on her desk and laid out an assortment of brushes. Standing back, she visualized the murals coming to life on the barren walls.

She started with a quote from Harry Potter along one wall, *Always*. The familiar words in her own handwriting made her smile. On the opposite wall, she painted a scene of Lucy and Aslan from The Lion, the Witch and the Wardrobe — one of the books she, Makenna, and Tristen had bonded over years ago when they were children running through the fields together.

Maddie worked steadily as the room transformed. She didn't notice the fading sunlight or hear her dad calling her for dinner. She was lost in her creative world, making this new space feel like home.

Maddie kept painting into the night, bringing the walls to life with splashes of color and imagination. She blended shades of blue for the ocean scene from The Island of the Blue Dolphins, using sweeping strokes to capture the motion of the waves. It had been one of Maddie's favorites before...

Maddie paused, brush in hand. Before Makenna got sick. They used to read together, act out scenes, and compare notes. A lump formed in Maddie's throat as she continued painting, trying to push the memories aside. Still, they crept in as she outlined lyrics from one of Makenna's favorite songs. Maddie could almost hear her sister's off-key singing and see her dancing goofily to the upbeat melody. Tears blurred Maddie's vision, dripping onto the unfinished mural.

She stepped back, taking a shaky breath. Looking around the room, it felt empty without Makenna there to appreciate it with her. Maddie sank down against the wall, letting the tears fall.

"I miss you," she whispered. For a moment, she felt Makenna's presence, her infectious laugh, her unwavering support.

Maddie stood, wiping her eyes. She picked up the brush again, determined to fill the room with light — for both her and Makenna.

The sun streamed in through the windows as Maddie put the finishing touches on the murals. She stepped back to admire her work — sweeping ocean scenes, lyrics from favorite songs, literary quotes, and a galaxy of glittering stars. It was a reflection of her inner world, brought to life on the walls.

A knock at the door made Maddie turn. She opened it to find her dad standing there, his eyes widening as he took in the room.

"Whoa," he exclaimed. "This is...amazing."

Maddie smiled shyly. "You really like it?"

"Are you kidding? It's incredible!" Her dad stepped inside, gazing around in awe. He paused at the ocean scene, taking in the swirling blues and greens. "It feels like I'm right there, on the waves."

Maddie nodded. "That one makes me feel peaceful. Like floating away."

Her father turned to the lyrics next, recognition lighting his face. "Our road trip song," he said with a grin.

Maddie laughed. "Yeah, Makenna used to play it nonstop." Her smile faltered for a moment before she added, "She would have loved this room."

Robert put a hand on his daughter's shoulder. "She's here, Maddie. In everything you create. She's so proud of you."

Maddie's eyes glistened with tears. But this time, they were tears of healing. Of finding light in the darkness. "Thank you, Dad."

They stood together, comforted by art and memory. Maddie knew then that they would face it together no matter what came next. "Do you think I can go to the library and check out a few books?" Maddie asked him unexpectedly.

"Sure, be back by dinner?"

"It's a deal." Maddie grabbed her backpack and headed out the door. She was only being half truthful with him. Maddie thoroughly planned to go to the library. She just didn't tell her dad that she was going to text Tristen to meet her there.

Maddie walked down the street, feeling a sense of nervous excitement that she couldn't shake. She kept replaying the plan in her head: text Tristen to meet her at the library, hide in the stacks until they were alone, confess her love and hope he felt the same. It was a bold, terrifying plan, but Maddie was prepared to execute it.

She stepped into the cool, quiet building, taking a deep breath and letting it out slowly. Maddie made her way to the back, scanning the bookshelves for Tristen's unruly hair or familiar frame. When she reached the secluded corner on the second floor, she found him sitting at a small round table with a stack of books in front of him.

Tristen looked up as she approached, and a slow smile spread across his face. "Hey."

"Hi," Maddie replied, her heart thudding in her chest. This was it. The moment of truth. Could she go through with it?

Tristen stood up, and Maddie's eyes traveled over his broad shoulders, down his lean torso, stopping at his worn jeans and scuffed work boots. He was dressed like usual-simple, functional clothing — yet he made it look like he'd just stepped off a fashion runway. Maddie felt a flush cross her cheeks as she realized how ridiculous she must look in comparison. She'd thrown on her favorite T-shirt and jeans without much thought.

Tristen placed his hand on her arm, pulling her close. "What's up?"

Maddie bit her lip, wondering if this was really such a good idea after all. Her mind flashed to all the reasons why they couldn't be together — the resentment between their fathers that had boiled over into town gossip, the disapproval of their relationship, the fear of hurting her father. Maddie wasn't even sure if Tristen had told his father about her at all. But then she looked into Tristen's warm blue eyes and felt a sense of peace wash over her.

"I need to tell you something," Maddie said, her voice barely above a whisper.

Tristen's expression softened. "Okay. What is it?"

Maddie took a deep breath and sat down next to him. She knew what she wanted to tell him, but at the last minute, she caved. "I care about you, Tristen."

There was a moment of silence as Tristen processed her words. Then he gently brushed his thumb over her cheek. "I care about you too, Maddie."

Relief flooded Maddie's body as Tristen leaned in to kiss her. His lips were warm and gentle against hers, sending sparks shooting through her body. Maddie closed her eyes and let herself get lost in the moment, forgetting everything but the feel of Tristen's arms around her, the taste of his lips on hers.

When they finally pulled away, Maddie felt like she was floating on air. He always made her feel that way. Did it always feel that way to kiss a boy? Maddie had no other reference for comparison, but she doubted it.

"We probably shouldn't do too much of that in here, though. The books have eyes," warned Tristen.

"I thought that was potatoes," teased Maddie.

"Could be, but seriously, the librarian is a friend of my dad's, so we can't be too careful here."

"Got it." Maddie picked up one of the books on the table and pretended to thumb through it.

Tristen leaned back in his chair and looked around as he casually changed the subject. "So, we're gonna be going to the same school now. That's pretty cool."

"Yeah, at least I'll know someone there." But would he be her boyfriend at school, or just love her on the side in secrecy the way they had all summer?

"We can compare schedules when we get them," Tristen said. "Maybe we'll have some classes together."

"I hope so." Maddie traced her finger over a few of the words in the book. "Everything is going to be so different now."

"Different can be good, though. You get to start fresh."

Maddie smiled slightly. "No more 'new kid' for me. That'll be nice."

"And you'll have a built-in guide to show you around," Tristen added with a grin.

Maddie laughed. "My own personal tour guide, huh?"

"Yep, I know all the best hang-out spots, the cool teachers, the ones to avoid."

They chuckled together, the prospect of a new school year feeling a little less daunting. Makenna only hoped people had forgotten what had gone down at the bonfire. She would probably never live that down.

"We're gonna have a great year," Tristen said, bumping her shoulder. "And we'll make sure Makenna's with us in spirit. Keeping you out of trouble."

Maddie rolled her eyes playfully. "Hey, I'm not the

troublemaker here."

They laughed again, the sound filling up the space around them. Maddie looked around at the shelves of books, half expecting someone to shush them into silence, but no warning came. She was glad she got to see Tristen for a little bit, even if they had to be super careful of their interactions. He told her he loved her, and Maddie was going to hang onto that for as long as she could.

As they gathered up their books and headed out of the library hand in hand, Maddie knew that Makenna was with her in spirit. She could almost hear her sister's voice whispering in her ear: "Go for it, Maddie. Follow your heart." And so she did.

Chapter 12

The first day of school was not off to a good start. Tristen wasn't in any of her morning classes so far, and he had been so late to school she hadn't even seen him. When she finally did get a peek at him, he was surrounded by all the football players and impossible to get his attention. Maddie felt a little lost and hurt by it all.

As Maddie walked through the crowded hallway, she couldn't help but feel like a small fish in an ocean of sharks. In the hallway, the other fish did whatever they could to ignore the cool school of fish that seemed to take up all the time and space. Everyone else was just little minnows trying not to be eaten alive by the power structure. She saw the football players huddled together, their red and white jerseys making them stand out from the sea of students dressed in blue and silver. Tristen was among them, laughing and joking around with his teammates.

Maddie couldn't help but feel a twinge of jealousy as she watched him from afar. She had been hoping to see him today, but it seemed like fate was against her. She wondered if he even knew that she existed inside these walls. This was definitely not the way she expected her first day to go down.

Maddie was lost in thought before a familiar voice broke through her reverie. "Well, if it isn't the new girl. How's your first day going?" asked Tiffany.

Maddie shrugged. "It's been okay so far. I haven't seen Tristen anywhere, though."

Tiffany rolled her eyes. "Girl, you need to get over him. You know it's never going to work out between you two with all the history between your families. Besides, he's a full on player."

"Thanks for the warning, but I can take care of myself," answered Maddie. She knew Tiffany was not looking out for her one bit. The girl was still annoyed that Tristen had decided not to go out with her.

"Don't say I didn't warn you."

Maddie sighed. Tiffany was probably right. It was going to be difficult for them to have a relationship with the way their families were split down the line. There was no love lost between the Tylers and the Grants. Their feud had transcended well past high school. Her father had never forgotten. Had Daniel Grant? Or was he even bothered by the memory since he was the instigator in this story? Did Tristen even know what kind of bully his father was?

The bell rang, and she was reminded that it was lunchtime. She made her way down the hallway to the cafeteria. The cafeteria was a hectic place. Piles of students were lined up, and Maddie had to maneuver through the crowd just to get her meal from the buffet line. She got a tray with some overcooked vegetables, processed chicken nuggets and white rice that looked like it came straight out of a paper bag; in short, school lunch food at its finest! She quickly grabbed her food before anyone could elbow their way past her into the ever-shrinking queue.

Once she made it back with her utensils in hand, Maddie went looking for an empty seat so she could sit down for lunch without having to stand awkwardly against one wall or another. That would have been excruciating, to say the least. After quite some searching about, she finally spotted one lone table tucked behind two pillars that emerged as an oasis amidst all this chaos — thankfully unoccupied by any living soul.

Maddie sat alone at a cafeteria table, poking at the unappetizing food on her tray. The buzz of chatter and laughter from the other students washed over her, a bitter reminder of her isolation. Ever since her twin had died, Maddie felt like an outsider everywhere she went. If Makenna were here right now, they would talk about all their classes and expound on each teacher and the various boring lectures they already had to endure. At least she could have counted on her.

She glanced around the cafeteria, taking in the groups of friends laughing together. A pang of loneliness hit her chest. More than anything, she wished she could be a part of one of those groups, to feel like she belonged somewhere.

"Hey loser!" a voice jeered, jolting Maddie from her thoughts. She looked up to see a group of popular girls smirking down at her.

"We're having a party this weekend," the ringleader, Tiffany, announced. "Don't even think about coming. It's invite only, and you're definitely NOT invited. We wouldn't want dear daddy showing up, would we?"

The girls cackled as they sashayed away. Maddie blinked back tears, humiliation burning through her. She knew Tiffany would strike out at her sometime. Guess her warning earlier wasn't the olive branch it had seemed to be.

"Mind if we sit here?" asked Lydia.

Maddie looked up to see a girl from one of her classes, Lydia. Lydia was standing next to a skinny boy who Maddie had never met before and another kid who she was having trouble figuring out the gender.

"Sure." Maddie waved to the seats across from her.

"I'm Lydia," the blonde girl said. "That's Thomas. And Jax."

The brooding boy with jet-black hair gave Maddie a nod. "Thomas."

"Jax, if you didn't already figure that out." Jax sat down and opened the carton of milk.

"I'm Maddie." Maddie cleared her throat and asked the question that was at the forefront of her mind. "Not to be rude, but can I ask..."

"I get it. You're new, so you don't know. The simplest answer is, my pronouns are they/them," interjected Jax.

"Oh. Okay. I'll do my best to remember that."

"Don't worry, if you forget, we'll help you remember," promised Lydia.

"Thanks. And thanks for joining me. Are you sure you want to take the risk?"

"It's not like we're at the top of the food chain here," answered Thomas. "We're lucky not to be chum."

"Chum?" asked Maddie.

"You know, the stuff they throw into the water to catch sharks?" answered Thomas.

Jax gestured to the loud, crowded tables of popular teens. "They're the sharks."

"Got it." It was a hierarchy that Maddie understood.

Maddie picked at her food, sneaking glances at her new tablemates. Lydia chatted brightly about an art project while Thomas nodded along, nose still in his book.

Jax sat silently, their brow furrowed as they doodled in a notebook. Maddie wondered what Jax was thinking about so intensely. She noticed their nails were painted black, and they wore several leather bracelets crowded with silver charms.

"So, Maddie," Lydia said, turning to her with a friendly smile. "What kind of stuff are you into?"

Maddie hesitated. No one had asked her that in a long time. "Art, painting," she said finally. "And astronomy. I have a telescope my dad got me for my birthday last year."

"That's awesome!" Lydia said. "We should totally go stargazing sometime."

Thomas finally looked up from his book. "I'm into astronomy too," he said quietly. "I know a good spot to see the Milky Way, away from the city lights."

"We should all go," Lydia declared. "Make it a night this weekend."

Maddie's heart swelled. It had been so long since she'd been invited anywhere. "I'd love that," she said, meeting Thomas' shy smile.

Jax capped the pen and stretched their arms over their head. "Yeah, I'm in," Jax said, turning to Maddie. Their green eyes were piercing. "Sounds like fun."

"Yeah. It does." Maddie was happy to have plans with friends. Outside of Tristen, she really didn't know anyone here. It would be nice to hang out with someone else for a change, especially with how busy Tristen was with football.

By the time lunch was over, she was in much better spirits. Maddie smiled to herself as she walked to her next class. She felt lighter than she had in a long time. For once, she was looking forward to the weekend instead of dreading two more days alone.

As she approached her locker, she noticed a group of girls clustered nearby. They fell silent and stared as Maddie unlocked her locker. She could feel their eyes burning into her back. Her stomach tightened. Maddie kept her eyes down as she switched out her books, trying to ignore them. But their whispers floated over.

"Ugh, did you see who she ate lunch with..."

"What a freak show."

"She's so desperate for friends she'll take anyone."

Maddie's face burned. She slammed her locker louder than she meant to. As she hurried away, she heard them erupt in giggles behind her. Hot tears stung her eyes as she escaped to the bathroom. She leaned against the sink, taking deep breaths. She wouldn't let them get to her, not today. Not when she finally had real friends. So what if they were a little awkward? Jax, Lydia and Thomas saw her — really saw her — in a way no one else did anymore. They didn't care about her dad or her past. All that mattered was who she was right now.

Maddie dabbed at her eyes, composing herself before heading to class. She wouldn't let anything ruin this feeling. For the first time in forever, she belonged with people who didn't question who she was, where she came from, or what kind of baggage she had brought along with her.

Maddie slid into her seat next to Lydia just as the bell rang.

"Cutting it close," Lydia said with a smirk.

"The cool kids seem to hate me," Maddie said. It was a joke that came out without thought, and the words hit her like a slap as soon as they were out of her mouth. What had she just said?

Lydia covered her mouth with her hands, but her eyes gave her away. She was laughing. "I don't know, Maddie. They'd have to be really dumb to not be into you."

As Lydia leaned in for a hug, a roar of laughter erupted from the back of the classroom. Maddie turned to see the band of girls who had given her so much grief at lunchtime standing in the doorway. The girls stared at Maddie and Lydia, then started shrieking with laughter as they joined their friends in the back row.

Thomas froze in his seat after checking his schedule. "This is today's circle of hell?" he asked under his breath.

Maddie nodded solemnly. This wasn't looking good at all. If those girls were going to be in this class, it was definitely going to be a long year.

Lydia stuck her tongue out at the girls before turning to

face Thomas and Jax next to her. A smile was fixed on her face as she quietly asked, "So, is anyone else dying to be here?"

Maddie tried to relax as she peeked over her shoulder at the still giggling girls behind them. One girl pantomimed something nasty as she whispered it to another, who snorted in response and then covered their mouth in fake embarrassment as they burst into laughter again. Maddie was still looking back when she saw Tristen enter the room. One small glimpse and her world seemed to right itself, especially when she saw him walking in their direction.

He stopped at the desk behind her. "This seat taken?"

"No, not at all," Maddie almost whispered.

"Wait, what? Don't tell me the hometown hero has decided to grace us with his presence," Thomas made a mock gasp.

"You're Thomas, right?" asked Tristen.

"He knows my name? Color me shocked." Thomas put a hand to his chest.

"Stop. You're just embarrassing yourself," chided Lydia. "You'll have to forgive him. He's a drama king. I'm Lydia."

"Right. We had Speech last year." Tristen added.

"Where were you today?" Maddie didn't have the patience to wait for her turn. His absence this morning had hurt her. Maddie was counting on him to help her get through the start at the new school. Instead, she had been alone, dealing with the fallout from the summer and all the mean girl drama that she was sure Tiffany was behind. Having him there wouldn't have stopped Tiffany and her goons, but seeing his smiling face would have been at least a consolation prize.

"Would you believe I overslept?" Tristen gave her a goofy grin.

"You? Never!" she teased him.

"My mom had to call me in so I wouldn't get a tardy." Tristen pulled out his binder and put it on his desk.

"What was her excuse?" asked Maddie.

"Family emergency." Tristen grinned.

"It's only the first day. Not like you missed much," interjected Lydia, who had been listening in.

At that moment, Mr. Angelo started to give his welcome to their history class.

"Welcome to American History. My name is Mr. Angelo, and I will be your teacher for the year..."

Maddie straightened in her seat, trying her best not to fidget. She kept her gaze trained on Mr. Angelo's face as he droned on about his course expectations and the year syllabus.

Jax was leaning against the wall behind Maddie. She noticed their hand absently pick up their pen and then put it down again. They were obviously bored, but a glance at Lydia showed they had given up bothering with what other people thought of them long ago.

Thomas, on the other side of Lydia, wasn't looking at Mr. Angelo either, instead contentedly staring at the girls behind them, seemingly unconcerned with both the giggling group's antics and Mr. Angelo's droning voice.

"Why don't we get started?" Mr. Angelo declared finally after passing out packets of worksheets. "Thomas, you can begin."

"If you say so," Thomas said hesitantly, his voice low as he read from the packet in front of him, his eyes glued to it the whole time.

For the next thirty minutes, the class read from the packet that Mr. Angelo passed out to them. Each of them took turns reading a section, something Maddie hadn't done since middle school. Soon after class began, Mr. Angelo passed by their desks with a stack of papers. "Here's some additional reading material for the week.

"Great. Looks like we have a crap ton of homework. Guess stargazing will have to come later," grumbled Lydia.

"That's ok. The stars will be there."

Maddie settled in for the rest of the class and started to take notes. Her father would never let her live it down if she didn't at least pull off a B average this year. No excuses, ever. Even when Makenna was sick, Maddie had to be extra perfect. Now that she was gone, Maddie was the only child left to focus on, and he was sure to double down.

The class passed quickly, followed by the next two, and before she knew it, the day was over. Her first day, and she only had two classes with Tristen. She wished they could spend more time together, but she would be happy for the time they had. All in all, the day had turned out to be okay if she factored out the cheer squad that was dedicated to making her life miserable. Maddie could only hope that it passed quickly, and they found another target to zero in on before the end of the month.

Chapter 13

Tristen stared at the faded photograph in his hand, a bittersweet reminder of simpler times. It showed him as a young boy, beaming with pride as his father ruffled his hair after a big win from the peewee football league. Those were the days when pleasing Dad was all that mattered, when Tristen's future seemed set in stone — become a star player, date the head cheerleader, be the big man on campus. He wanted nothing more than to play football and make his dad proud. But he also longed for the freedom to follow his heart, even if it meant jeopardizing their picture-perfect future.

Tristen slid the photo back into his wallet with a sigh. He knew his father would be disappointed if he found out the truth — that Tristen's heart now belonged to Maddie Tyler, the quiet girl who always sat alone at lunch. She wasn't a cheerleader or from the popular crowd. In fact, she was still grieving the recent loss of her twin sister to leukemia. But none of that mattered to Tristen. When he was with Maddie, all the superficial high school drama faded away. She saw him as more than just the coach's son or the star quarterback. She truly understood him.

Lately, their conversations had taken on a new intimacy. Maddie confessed her grief over losing her sister and the pressure she felt to be strong for her parents. Tristen opened up about his strained relationship with his dad and the future that had been decided for him. Their shared pain brought them closer together.

Tristen longed to tell his father how he felt, to explain that he was questioning the rigid expectations that had been ingrained in him since childhood. But he could already imagine the disapproval etched on his dad's face, the accusations of betrayal tossed in anger. No, he couldn't reveal his feelings, not yet. For now, his blossoming relationship with Maddie would have to remain a bittersweet secret.

Tristen knew that his feelings for Maddie were growing beyond friendship. The thought thrilled and terrified him. He had never wanted someone the way he wanted her. But pursuing that desire would mean turning his life upside down. Was she worth the risk? As Tristen watched her tuck a strand of chestnut hair behind her ear, he knew his answer.

It didn't help that there was some lowkey rivalry between their dads. Tristen had never heard his father speak of Robert Tyler before, but apparently, there was beef there, one that Maddie's dad had not gotten over. He was tempted to ask what had happened between them, but was afraid of what the answer would be. Tristen knew his father was a hothead. He'd heard him talk about the good old days a few times, where being the star player and homecoming king had been his most important accomplishments. Tristen's father didn't seem like the kind of person to let anyone stand in his way. How many people had he stepped on along the way?

Tristen slid his phone back into his pocket, avoiding the ten missed calls from Tiffany. Ever since he and Maddie had started spending more time together, he'd been dodging Tiffany's texts and calls. He knew he should deal with her and let her down gently for the second time since that summer, but he just didn't feel up to her games right now.

Tristen arrived at the bleachers for football practice, bracing himself for the barrage of bro hugs and macho banter.

His best friend Derek approached with a mischievous grin.

"Yo, T! Smash any babes this weekend?" Derek hooted. The other guys hooted and hollered.

Tristen faked a smile. He knew Derek hadn't smashed anything. He was just pretending to be something he wasn't. Tristen was getting tired of putting up some lame front to the rest of the world. Why did everyone else expect him to be a player only looking to score with some chick? It really wasn't his thing. Maybe it's what his father expected of him, but it wasn't who Tristen wanted to be.

"You know me, just focused on the game," he replied, even as his thoughts drifted to the milkshakes he shared with Maddie over the summer. Their relationship was simple: no expectations of how he should act or what he should be. Maddie liked him for who he was without all these prying eyes watching his every move.

"That's the spirit!" bellowed Coach Stevens, the head football coach. "No distractions from the prize." He gave Tristen's shoulder an approving squeeze.

"Glad to hear you're focused on the game," came another voice.

Tyler turned to see Robert Tyler had joined them on the field. Tristen's heart sank when he saw the way the new coach sized him up and seemed to find him lacking. "Yes, sir."

Coach Stevens gestured to the team. "Boys, I'd like you to meet our new assistant coach, Robert Tyler."

Tristen watched as his father's old rival approached the team with a smug expression on his face. He could tell that Coach Tyler was sizing them up, trying to find any weaknesses in their defenses. Tristen clenched his fists, suddenly feeling more determined than ever to beat their rivals in the upcoming season.

"Good to be here," Coach Tyler said, straightening his

jacket. "I'm looking forward to working with this talented group of young men."

Tristen bit back a snort. He knew that his father and Robert Tyler's rivalry went deeper than just high school football games. But he felt a twinge of guilt when he saw Maddie watching from the sideline, her eyes following him with concern.

"Time to run a few plays," Coach Stevens ordered the team.

Tristen took his position on the field. He couldn't shake the feeling that Coach Tyler was watching him more closely than the others. He glanced over at Maddie, who was sitting in the stands with her notebook and pen in hand, ready to analyze every move they made. As he caught her eye, he saw the worry etched on her face and gave her a small smile to reassure her.

The scrimmage began, and Tristen could feel his muscles strain as he sprinted towards his opponents. His focus was on the game until he heard the sound of someone shouting his name from the sidelines. He looked up to see Tiffany, arms crossed and glaring at him.

"What's going on with you, Tristen? You're ignoring my calls and texts."

Tristen sighed inwardly. There was just no easy way to handle Tiffany's drama. "I think we should talk later," he said, hoping to appease her for now.

As he resumed playing, his mind drifted back to Maddie. He knew he was taking a risk by pursuing a relationship with her. Their fathers' rivalry was just one of many obstacles. But Maddie was worth it — every stolen moment with her was like finding a hidden gem.

After practice ended, Tristen was walking back to the locker room when Coach Tyler approached him.

"Can I have a word with you, Tristen?"

Tristen nodded warily. Was this about their fathers' rivalry? Or had he messed up during practice? Tristen found himself second-guessing every second now.

"Listen, Tristen," Coach Tyler said in a low voice. "I know our families have some history, but I don't want that to get between us or affect your playing on the field. You are a talented athlete, and I hope to work with you to bring out your full potential."

Tristen was taken aback by the unexpected words of encouragement from his father's rival. He could see a genuine interest in Coach Tyler's eyes that he had never seen before, and he felt himself let go of some of his underlying resentment.

"Thank you, Coach," Tristen said, feeling a bit more at ease. "I'll do my best."

As Tristen continued walking away from Coach Tyler, he made up his mind to give him a chance. Maybe there was more to their fathers' story than just a high school rivalry. Tristen couldn't help but wonder what had happened between them all those years ago.

He walked past Maddie on the sideline and could see her smile at him with relief. It was as if she could sense that things had gone well between him and Coach Tyler.

Tristen knew they were taking a risk by being together, but their connection was too strong to ignore. His feelings for Maddie were real. He wanted to talk to her about what he was feeling — the pressure from his dad to be the perfect son and star athlete and the guilt over falling for someone that he shouldn't be with. But before he could say anything, Tiffany interrupted with her jealous tirade.

Tristen turned his attention to Tiffany, trying to defuse the situation before it got out of hand. "Tiffany, can we talk later? I'm a bit tired from practice," he said, hoping to buy himself some time.

Tiffany huffed and crossed her arms. "Fine. But we

need to talk."

Tristen nodded, relieved that he had dodged a bullet for now. He turned back to Maddie, who was still watching him with a concerned expression. He walked over to her and took her hand in his.

"Hey," he said, looking deeply into her eyes. "I just wanted to say that I'm glad you were here watching me today."

Maddie smiled softly at him. "Of course, I was here. I wouldn't miss it for the world."

They stood there for a moment, lost in their own world. Tristen felt like he could stay there forever, just holding Maddie's hand. But he knew they couldn't stay like this forever — they had to face the reality of their situation at some point.

"I need to talk to you about something," Tristen said finally.

Maddie's expression turned serious. "What is it?"

Tristen hesitated, not sure how to put his feelings into words. "I just...I feel like we're taking a huge risk by being together," he said finally. "Our dads' rivalry isn't going away anytime soon, and I don't want that to affect us."

Maddie squeezed his hand reassuringly. "I know it's risky, but I believe in us," she said firmly.

Tristen felt a sudden rush of emotion, his heart pounding in his chest as he looked at her. "I believe in us too," he said, feeling renewed determination to make their relationship work.

Maddie leaned in and kissed him, her lips soft and sweet against his. Tristen kissed her back passionately, lost in the moment. But as they broke apart, they both knew that their love was forbidden. They had to be careful to keep their relationship a secret from their families and the rest of the world.

Tristen pulled Maddie into a hug, not wanting to let go. He knew that every moment with her was precious, and he was willing to risk everything for her. As they embraced, Tristen couldn't shake the feeling that something big was about to happen. Something that would change everything. But for now, all he wanted was to be with Maddie. To love her and protect her, no matter what.

"So, what do you think of Coach Tyler?" she asked, twirling a strand of hair around her finger.

Tristen hesitated. "He's fine, I guess," he shrugged. "Just another person trying to tell me who I should be."

Maddie smiled sympathetically. "I know how it feels," she said softly. "My dad wants me to be someone I'm not too."

Tristen took Maddie's hand, feeling a rush of warmth spread through him at the contact. "I don't want to be someone I'm not," he said firmly. "I want to be with you, Maddie. But there's so much standing in our way."

Maddie looked up at him, her eyes filled with understanding. "I know," she said quietly. "But I also know that we can't keep pretending that what we feel for each other isn't real."

Tristen felt a wave of relief wash over him — he wasn't alone in this. "So what do we do?" he asked.

Maddie took a deep breath. "We keep it a secret for now," she said firmly. "Until we figure out a way to make people see that what we have is real."

Tristen nodded, feeling a sense of determination set in. He didn't know how they would make it work — especially with their fathers' old rivalry still lingering in the background — but he knew that he wasn't going to give up on Maddie.

As they walked away from the school building, hand in hand, Tristen couldn't help but feel like they were walking toward something bigger than just their love for each other. They were walking towards a future where they could be who they wanted to be and love who they wanted to love without fear of judgment or ridicule.

Chapter 14

School started to fade into a normal everyday routine. For Maddie, it had become a sanctuary where she could pretend to be someone else entirely. There, she did not have to carry her grief every second of the day. She could set it aside and compartmentalize a little more each day. Her friends were a great help in that department. In fact, they had finally made a plan to go stargazing together.

When Maddie asked her parents if she could go stargazing with her new friends, she was afraid they would say no. They had surprised her, though, giving her their trust. It had taken just a few minute's deliberation for them to say yes. The fact that she was only going with friends made their answer easier to come by. Her parents were glad that Maddie was making friends and settling into school.

The four of them headed to the nature preserve to get as far away from town as possible. The preserve was close to the Mellow Creek Caverns. The four of them had already been hiking to find the perfect spot to stargaze. At this point, Maddie was ready to collapse from the hike. Maddie plopped down onto a mossy boulder, wiping sweat from her brow. Her calves burned from the steep incline of the hike.

"I'm ready to keel over," she panted.

Lydia sat down beside her, massaging her thighs. "No joke. My legs feel like jelly."

Jax and Thomas emerged from the trail, chests heaving. Thomas had volunteered to carry Maddie's telescope up the path. He set it down on the ground and took a breath. "Piece of cake."

"Are you kidding? That was brutal," Jax wheezed, hands on their knees.

Maddie gazed at her exhausted friends, a weary smile touching her lips. At first, Thomas just wanted to go to the small viewing area near the parking lot. It had been Maddie's idea to come to the meadow, mostly because it had been one of her sister's favorite spots. Maddie still wanted to be anywhere that Makenna felt closer to her. She would never write her out of her life.

Maddie froze in place, her lips parted slightly, and her eyes glazed over with emotion. She thought about her sister — Makenna — and felt a wave of nostalgia and love wash over her. She remembered the night they had spent stargazing together, their laughter echoing off the walls of the meadow. She remembered how they had laid out a blanket and bundled up in jackets as night descended over them. Their parents were there, too, keeping a watchful eye over their girls. Maddie's eyes lit up when Makenna pointed out all the constellations — holding her finger in each position for an eternity to make sure she memorized their shapes and stories.

They had galivanted across the meadow, searching for shooting stars, sharing oversized bags of popcorn and singing along to every song that played on the radio until their voices were hoarse from fatigue. Even after they ran out of battery power on both of their phones, neither one stopped taking in the different shapes or taking turns spinning around with arms stretched wide open like starfish catching air currents beneath waves crashing onto shorelines. The beauty of it all stung Maddie's chest with heartache yet filled it simultaneously with joyous reminiscence.

Lydia suddenly perked up. "Hey, we're not far from that meadow. We should get some good stargazing in tonight!"

Thomas nodded eagerly. "You got the snacks?"

"Sure do," Lydia patted her backpack.

Lydia's enthusiasm was infectious. "Yeah, let's do it," Maddie said finally.

"Awesome!" Lydia sprang up, reenergized. "Lead the way, Maddie."

The group gathered their gear and set off down the trail, bantering lightheartedly. But an undercurrent of melancholy still clung to Maddie's heart. Gazing at the darkening sky, she sent a silent message to her sister. 'I miss you, Kenna. But I'm learning to live again.'

The meadow opened up before them, a sea of lush grass rimmed by trees. Crickets chorused loudly as the group made their way to the clearing's edge. Maddie inhaled, taking in the way the pine and earth around her. A gentle breeze ruffled her hair. Above, the inky sky was splattered with stars. She knew it was going to be a night she would never forget.

"This is perfect," Lydia declared, dropping her backpack.

Jax and Thomas began unpacking the telescopes and binoculars. Maddie helped Lydia smooth out blankets and pillows on the ground.

Lydia gave her a sympathetic smile. "How are you holding up?"

"I'm okay," Maddie replied. "It's hard, but...I know Kenna would want this. For me to keep living."

Lydia squeezed her hand. "I wish I could have known her, too."

"She would have loved you all." Maddie smiled at Lydia.

Soon, they were bundled up on the blankets, peering skyward. Maddie pointed out the Milky Way, tracing the hazy band with her finger. She snapped a photo and sent it to Tristen, wondering what he was up to now. Maddie hadn't really heard much from him today, but that was okay. It wasn't like she sat by her phone, dying to hear something from him. They both had their own lives outside of their relationship.

"There's Orion," Thomas said, adjusting the telescope. "One of the clearest constellations."

Maddie leaned back, listening to her friends' chatter. A shooting star suddenly blazed overhead. Maddie closed her eyes, letting the sounds of the night wash over her. The breeze rustling the trees, her friends' murmured conversation, the distant hoot of an owl, all of it created an enchanted backdrop to a night she would never forget. She thought of all the times she and Makenna had lain beneath these very stars, dreaming up constellations and whispering secrets. Her throat tightened, memories of stargazing with Makenna rising up inside her again. The way Makenna would gasp and point whenever a meteor appeared, the times she would make a wish for some insane request...

Makenna had always been the first to spot a shooting star. "Make a wish, Mad!" she'd cry excitedly, squeezing Maddie's hand. Maddie wished for the same thing every time — for her sister's health, for just a few more days together.

Now, when she saw a shooting star, Maddie wasn't sure what to wish for. Life without Makenna still felt unreal, like she'd drifted into some alternate universe. One where she gazed at the stars alone. A tear slipped down Maddie's cheek. She wiped it away hurriedly as Jax glanced over.

"You okay?" they asked gently.

Maddie nodded, managing a shaky smile. "Yeah. Just thinking about her."

Jax's expression softened with understanding. They

patted her shoulder. "We're here for you, Mad. However you need."

"I know," Maddie whispered. "Thank you."

She sat up straighter, taking a deep breath. Kenna was here, written in the stars above. As long as Maddie kept her memory close, she could make it through this unfathomable loss. One day at a time, one breath at a time. She pushed the memories away for now, focusing on this moment under the stars with her friends. Makenna was here in spirit. And someday, Maddie knew, they would gaze at the same sky again.

After a while, the night chill settled in. Maddie yawned and put away her phone. "Guess it's time to head back," she said reluctantly. The others nodded, beginning to gather their things in silence; they all felt Makenna's absence like a third person here with them tonight.

The sky had begun to lighten by the time they returned home, still talking quietly about Makenna and what she would think of this meadow visit if she were here today. As always, wishing that life could be different was futile. Nothing could change the path before her. It had already seemed to be predetermined. Losing Makenna was one fork in the road, one that could not be avoided no matter how hard they had tried. At least on this path, she wasn't completely alone. She waved goodbye as everyone went off on their way, but instead of heading into her house, Maddie snuck off to the one place that called to her. Their tree.

Maddie stopped outside the tree and set the telescope near the base. She ran her hand over its bark, gently remembering how Makenna used to climb up and sit at the top of it when she wanted some alone time. It had been their special spot when they were younger — telling secrets underneath its branches until dawn rose in spectacular shades of pink and orange.

Now, standing beneath it nearly brought Maddie to tears; everything reminded her so much of Makenna that she couldn't bear to be alone here any longer without breaking down altogether right there on this path. The memories echoed in rustling leaves overhead like whispers from another lifetime entirely. Her memory was never fully forgotten, no matter what else came or went through any of Maddie's living days. The twins would always be deeply rooted together like ancient trees connected by shared veins, their trunks reaching toward infinity where only the light could touch them. And when they both reached infinity, then the ultimate grand reunion would finally culminate in a reunion of lost souls. If wishes could create destiny, then Maddie was guaranteed to see her sister again. "I wish Heaven wasn't so far away. I miss you, Kenna."

Maddie sat by the tree, lost in thought, gazing up at the glittering night sky, when she heard the crunch of footsteps on the dry leaves behind her. She turned to see Tristen approaching, a bouquet of wildflowers in his hand.

"Hey, Maddie," he said softly. "Mind if I join you?"

Maddie smiled and patted the ground next to her. "Not at all."

Tristen settled down, placing the flowers in her lap. "Saw these near the fields. Thought you might like them."

"They're beautiful, thank you." Maddie brought them to her nose, inhaling the sweet scent.

They sat in comfortable silence for a few moments, shoulders barely touching. A light breeze rustled the leaves above them. Somewhere in the distance, an owl hooted its lonesome call.

"How are you doing?" Tristen asked finally. "Today must've brought up a lot of memories."

Maddie nodded, fingers trailing over the wildflowers. "It did. But mostly good ones. Me and Kenna spent so many nights under the stars, dreaming up constellations, telling stories..." Her voice caught.

Tristen slid his hand over hers and gave it a gentle squeeze. "I'm sure she's up there now, smiling down at you."

Maddie looked up at the glittering expanse of stars. "I hope so."

She leaned her head on Tristen's shoulder. He wrapped an arm around her, holding her close. And together, they gazed up at the heavens, taking comfort in each other's presence. Maddie was comforted by his presence. He always made her feel safe.

Maddie pointed up at the sky. "See those three bright stars in a row? Kenna and I called that the Princess Belt."

Tristen scanned the sky. "Ah yes, I see it now. Very creative."

"Thanks," Maddie said with a small laugh. "We made up all sorts of silly names when we were kids."

She adjusted her position, curling into Tristen's side. He responded by tightening his arm around her.

"What about you?" she asked. "Any favorite constellations?"

"Well, Orion is a classic. It's one of the easiest to spot." He traced the familiar belt and sword in the air.

Maddie followed the pattern with her eyes. "Right, of course. The mighty hunter."

"And you can't forget the Big Dipper," Tristen went on, pointing to the ladle-shaped grouping. "That one guided many an explorer."

"Mm, very true," Maddie murmured. She let her gaze drift across the rest of the sky. "It's crazy to think people used these stars to navigate across oceans and continents."

"It really is," Tristen agreed.

They sat without speaking for a minute, absorbing the serenity of the night. A light breeze rustled the trees around them. Somewhere in the distance, an owl hooted again.

Finally, Tristen broke the silence. "You know, staring up at the stars like this...it makes me think about the future."

Maddie turned to look at him. "What do you mean?"

"Just that...the possibilities seem endless. We could go anywhere, do anything." He gave her a meaningful look. "Together."

Maddie's heart fluttered. "I'd like that," she whispered.

Tristen smiled and pulled her close again. Maddie rested her head on his chest, listening to the steady rhythm of his heartbeat. Whatever the future held, she knew they would face it side by side, just like the endless sea of stars above them.

Chapter 15

Maddie tapped her pen impatiently against the library table, glancing at the clock. 2:15. Tristen was already 15 minutes late. Did he realize how much she had to tiptoe around the details here? Her dad had grilled her left and right to find out why she needed to go to the library and who her partner was. She had to make up a name so he wouldn't be too suspicious. If he knew that Maddie was planning to meet Tristen here, he would have locked her in her room.

She sighed and looked back down at her textbook, the glossy pages open to a chapter on Antietam. Not the most exciting topic, but certainly relevant to her own history. If only Daniel Grant hadn't acted like an ignorant imbecile so many years ago. The world hadn't changed a lot since the eighties, but had it changed enough for these two men to let their differences go? Probably not. People were often set in their ways, and change was something foreign to them.

It wasn't foreign to Maddie, though. Her life had gone through many stages in just the past few months. Grief, loss, survival. They all intermingled until sometimes Maddie couldn't tell the difference between each emotion. The only comfort she had was the normalcy that her friends and Tristen both brought to her life. She was not about to give any of them up anytime soon. Maddie didn't care what her father said.

The library door creaked open, and Maddie looked

up to see Tristen shuffling in, headphones around his neck and backpack slung over one shoulder. She felt a flare of annoyance. How could he be so lackadaisical about this project when their grades depended on it? And why didn't he at least text her that he was going to be late?

"Hey," he mumbled, dropping into the seat across from her.

Maddie pressed her lips together. "You're late."

Tristen shrugged, avoiding her gaze as he rifled through his backpack. Maddie studied the dark circles under his eyes and the slump in his shoulders. There was something defeated in his demeanor that gave her pause. Her irritation dissipated as she realized there must have been trouble on the home front again. She let it go, though, because his brooding eyes told her he wasn't ready to talk about it.

"Did you get a chance to look at the study guide I sent you?" she asked gently.

Tristen shook his head, staring down at the table. "Not yet."

Maddie waited, sensing there was more he wanted to say. The silence stretched between them. A librarian pushed a squeaky cart past.

"I've never been a fan of history," Tristen finally admitted.

Maddie nodded. She thought of her sister Makenna, who had always helped her study. The familiar ache of grief bloomed in her chest.

"Me either, but we'll get through it together," promised Maddie.

Tristen met her eyes then. After a moment, the corner of his mouth quirked up in a hint of a smile. Maddie found herself smiling back. Maddie pulled out her laptop and opened it, the glow of the screen reflecting on her face. "Here, take a look."

Tristen scooted his chair around to her side of the table so they could both look at the screen. His shoulder was almost close enough to touch hers. Maddie felt a warmth spread through her just being near him. That sickly, sweet, lovesick feeling almost distracted her from what she was about to say until she saw the file open on her screen. She blinked and brought herself back to reality.

"Okay, so I made this timeline of key Civil War battles," she said, pointing to the document on the screen. "I thought we could each focus on researching a different battle and presenting on it."

Tristen nodded, scrolling through the timeline. "Cool. Can I take Gettysburg? I think I remember some stuff about that from middle school."

"Sure," Maddie said. She was impressed he had retained anything from previous years. To Maddie, most of it was a blur of hospital visits.

As Tristen delved deeper into his own research, Maddie found herself distracted by the way his hair flopped around his face as he read. She couldn't help but stare at the way his eyes scanned the articles on his screen, the muscle in his jaw that twitched when he concentrated too hard. She remembered the last time they were together, the way Tristen's lips had felt against hers. It was dangerous, forbidden even, but Maddie couldn't help herself.

Tristen looked up from his screen and caught her staring. He raised an eyebrow, a small smile playing at the corner of his lips. "What?"

Maddie cleared her throat, averting her gaze. "Nothing."

But it wasn't nothing. She felt herself blush, embarrassed at how transparent she was being. Why couldn't she just play it cool? Every time he was near her, all she could do was think of him. Did she affect him the same way?

"I'm going to go grab a drink," Tristen announced, packing up his stuff. "You want anything?"

Maddie shook her head, pulling out her notebook to start taking notes. She could feel Tristen's absence like a physical ache as he walked away from the table. She didn't know how much longer she could keep pretending that this was just about schoolwork. To her, it was so much more than that. All week, she waited just for one moment to be near him without anyone else muddying the waters. It was too bad the time they spent had to be laden with homework and boring projects.

Maddie's mind wandered as she wrote down notes about Antietam. She knew her feelings for Tristen were foolish and impractical, but she couldn't help herself. There was something magnetic about him that drew her in, regardless of the consequences. She felt like she was playing with fire, but at the same time, she couldn't resist the temptation.

Maddie's thoughts were interrupted by the sound of Tristen returning to the table. He set a can of soda in front of her and sat down close enough to touch her again. Maddie couldn't help but shiver at the proximity.

"So, what did I miss?" he asked, his eyes glinting with amusement.

Maddie shrugged, trying to act nonchalant. "Just taking notes on Antietam."

Tristen nodded, taking a swig from his own drink. They worked in silence for a while longer until Maddie's phone buzzed on the table. She glanced at it to see a message from her dad.

"Looks like my time is running up. I got another hour tops," Maddie said abruptly, gathering her things.

"We better make the most of it then."

Maddie sighed as she stared at the half-finished outline on her laptop screen. They looked at the mess of books and papers spread around them. There was still a lot of work to do on their project, and the deadline was in two days. They had been working diligently for the past hour, but her heart just wasn't in it anymore. Ever since her dad's odd reaction to Tristen's last name, an invisible wedge had come between them.

Maddie let out a resigned sigh. "I wish we had more time."

"Me too." Tristen leaned back in his chair and scrubbed a hand over his face.

Maddie's eyes lingered on the way his muscles flexed under his t-shirt. She shook her head, trying to clear her thoughts. This wasn't the time or place for those kind of thoughts.

Tristen caught her staring, and she felt heat rise to her cheeks.

"What are you thinking about?" he asked, a playful glint in his eye.

Maddie hesitated, not wanting to admit the truth. "Just how much work we have left to do."

Tristen rolled his eyes. "Come on, Maddie. You can tell me anything."

Maddie took a deep breath and looked into his eyes. "I'm thinking about you, Tristen."

"I'm thinking about you too." Tristen leaned in to kiss her.

It was a soft, tentative kiss at first. Maddie's heart raced as she kissed him back, all her senses heightened. She ran her hands through his hair as the kiss deepened. Finally, they pulled back, eyes shining as they caught their breath.

Maddie looked around her to make sure no one had seen them. "The books..."

"Have eyes," finished Tristen with a secret smile.

"I wish we didn't have to hide so much." Maddie

glanced down at her hands and let out a disappointed sigh.

"Someday, that will change. We just have to keep the faith," promised Tristen. He reached his hand out to caress her face. "I've wanted to kiss you since I walked in the door."

"Me too," Maddie admitted. She rested her head on his shoulder. "What are we going to do about our parents, though? They'd freak if they knew."

Tristen wrapped his arms around her reassuringly. "We'll figure it out. All that matters is how we feel about each other. We can't let them keep us apart."

Maddie nodded, comforted by his words. As long as they had each other, she felt like they could handle anything. She tilted her face up for another kiss, thinking happily that this was just the beginning for them.

A ding on the phone interrupted her. "Great. I'm turning into a pumpkin even earlier."

"Cinderella must return to her humble abode?" asked Tristen.

"Something like that. I'll text you later."

"Same." Tristen nodded slowly, watching as Maddie packed up her things and headed out of the library.

As she walked away, Maddie couldn't help but feel frustrated and trapped. She wished that things could be simple between them, but she knew that it would never be that way. For now, all she could do was bury her feelings and focus on the project at hand. But as she walked out of the library, Maddie couldn't shake the feeling that she was playing a dangerous game. She just hoped that she wouldn't get burned in the end.

As she walked out of the library, Maddie wondered how her sister would handle this situation with her father. Would she fight with their dad, or would she give Tristen up? Maddie pushed the thought of her sister away and focused on walking home. The crisp autumn air did little to clear her head as she replayed the kiss with Tristen over and over again. She couldn't believe how much she wanted him, how much she craved his touch. This wasn't just a high school crush; this was something deeper, something more dangerous.

When Maddie arrived home, she found her dad in the living room, flipping through TV channels. He looked up when she walked in."Hey, kiddo. How was studying?"

Maddie tried to hide her flustered state, but she could feel a blush creeping up her neck. "It was good. We got a lot done."

Maddie was relieved when he didn't ask her for another word. Her cover was safe for now.

Chapter 16

Maddie smiled as the warm fall air caressed her skin. She had already changed out of her church clothes before heading to the nearby bowling alley to bowl with her friends. As she approached closer to the building, faint cheers from fellow bowlers reached Maddie's ears. That was enough to make Maddie feel even more excited about what lay ahead of them. She couldn't remember the last time she had gone bowling. It seemed like a lifetime ago.

Maddie propped open one of the double doors leading into The Ten Pin Alleyway Lanes — so named because it had only ten pins instead of fifteen due to its size. She squinted as sunlight beamed inside from windows painted with multi-colored pinwheels that shimmered against them. The inside smelled like fried food mixed with sweat. Laughter was ringing throughout while players tried their luck at strikes or spares on each lane, flickering under bright blue lights above each set-up.

Maddie went to the counter to pay for her game and rent a pair of shoes. Then she made her way over to the lane where her friends had already settled in. Maddie slid into the cracked vinyl seat of the bowling alley, the chatter of her friends washing over her. The balls crashed and thundered down the lanes, nostalgic rock music blaring from the speakers. Maddie glanced around at the familiar faces — Jax,

Thomas, and her best friend, Lydia.

She wished her sister was here to bowl with her in this cozy bowling alley. The noise from the players arguing over their ball selections of lanes for strikes and spares or reliving fabulous shots was a familiar sound from childhood times at the bowling alley. It had been years since she'd bowled, and it felt strange being back on the familiar plastic lane with its worn polish. She rested her fingers upon the cold, smooth surface of the ball as she set it down on the ball return. She felt the rising smoke of vapor billowing from the burners beneath her ball.

All was not lost, though. Maddie had a plan to make this day even better. Maddie sat down and checked her phone. Any minute now. The entrance chimed, and Maddie's breath caught. Tristen. His blue eyes found hers across the crowded alley. Maddie's heart fluttered as she waved him over.

"Hey!" Lydia followed Maddie's gaze, surprise flickering across her face. "I didn't know he was joining us."

Maddie bit her lip. "Last minute thing. I hope that's okay?"

Lydia shrugged, her ponytail swishing. "As long as he brought the goods."

Maddie smiled in return, but it didn't reach her eyes. If only Lydia knew. Knew why Maddie's father forbade her from seeing Tristen. Knew the secret rendezvous Maddie orchestrated, just for a glimpse of him. For now, she'd settle for a day of bowling. A day of normalcy.

Tristen slid next to Maddie, squeezing her hand beneath the table. "Hey," he murmured.

Maddie's chest loosened. With him by her side, she could breathe again. "Hey."

Maddie laced up her bowling shoes, her fingers fumbling over the laces. She could feel Tristen's eyes on her, patient and unwavering. Her heart fluttered. She finished tying her shoes and stood.

Tristen was already waiting, ball in hand. "You ready?"

Maddie nodded, grabbing her own ball. She followed him to the lane, hyperaware of his presence beside her. The sounds of the alley enveloped them — pins crashing, balls thudding, laughter and chatter. But all she could focus on was him.

Tristen bowled first, his form fluid and smooth. "Strike!"

"Nice!" Maddie was impressed.

"Your turn," he said, gesturing her forward.

Maddie positioned herself at the line, knees bent, ball weighed in her hands. She inhaled and swung her arm back. As she released the ball, her fingers stuck, and it veered left, only knocking down 7 pins.

"Nice try," Tristen said.

Maddie sighed, brushing a lock of hair from her face. "I used to be better at this."

Before her diagnosis. Before hospital beds and vomiting and bald heads. Back when her family was whole. She grabbed her ball for a second try, staring down the remaining pins. This time, when she rolled, a spare.

Tristen whistled. "There it is."

Maddie grinned her first real smile in weeks. For this one night, it was just her and her friends. The rest could wait. Maddie turned to head back to her seat but paused when she saw Lydia watching them. Her friend's eyes were hard, lips pressed in a firm line.

Maddie approached cautiously. "Hey Lydia, is everything okay?"

Lydia crossed her arms. "I didn't realize this was supposed to be a date."

Maddie flushed. "It's not — I just —"

"You should have told me you were using me as your

cover story," Lydia said sharply.

Maddie winced. She hadn't meant to deceive Lydia, but she knew her dad would never approve of Tristen.

"I'm sorry," Maddie said earnestly. "I didn't want you to feel uncomfortable. But I'm not ready to tell my dad yet. He'd probably kill me."

Lydia's expression softened slightly. She nodded in understanding. "It's okay, Maddie. I get it."

Maddie smiled, relieved. She knew Lydia would come around.

Tristen approached them, tentative. "Hey, Lydia. I'm really glad I could join you guys." He held out a hand.

Lydia eyed it warily before shaking. "Yeah, well, just don't try anything with Maddie while I'm around."

Tristen blinked, then chuckled. "Wouldn't dream of it."

"Alright, lovebirds. I'll play nice for one night. Next time, ask?" Lydia's expression softened. She stood and grabbed a bowling ball. "Now, let's bowl. Loser buys pizza."

"That will probably be me," added Maddie. Maddie smiled, relief flooding through her. With Lydia on their side, the day shone with possibility. A few stolen hours of normalcy and laughter. For now, it was enough.

"Don't count Jax out. They like the gutter zone," teased Thomas.

"Do not. It's not my fault that the balls seem to have a predetermined course. I swear they're plotting against me." Jax shrugged their shoulders.

Tristen stood up for his turn. He winked at Maddie before bowling a spare. "Yes!"

"Not bad," Lydia said, a hint of admiration in her voice.

Maddie grabbed a bowling ball, running her fingers over the smooth surface. She stepped up to the lane, drew back her arm, and let the ball fly. It crashed into the pins with a satisfying clatter.

"Strike!" Jax cheered. "Looks like I will get stuck buying pizza."

"Better you than me. Nice one, Maddie!" Thomas reached out his hand for a high-five.

Maddie grinned and high-fived Thomas. She was glad the tension from earlier seemed to have dissipated. Her group of friends had accepted Tristen at school, but they had not spent time outside of school with him, and part of that was the fact that Tristen was always in practice or other football activities. It kept him in his other group of friends, which made it awkward for Maddie and her friends at times. It was better to keep those parts of their lives separate.

They continued bowling, laughing and joking together. Maddie cherished these simple moments with her friends. For a little while, she could forget about everything else and just be a normal teenager. The dark clouds faded away, and all the holes that wanted to swallow her up hovered above her instead of constantly pulling her off her center of gravity. Maddie felt balanced and normal.

When Tristen bowled, Maddie found herself watching the way his arm muscles flexed beneath his t-shirt. A warmth spread through her chest that had nothing to do with the nachos they were sharing. At one point, their fingers brushed as they both reached for a chip. Maddie's heart raced at the contact. Yes, her feelings for Tristen were growing. And her friends seemed to be accepting it. She caught Lydia glancing between her and Tristen, a knowing look in her eyes.

The group treated Tristen like he was one of them. They razzed him if he missed the pins, or heaven forbid his ball dipped into the gutter alley. Maddie wished every day could be like this. When he got a strike, everyone cheered.

"Nice one, man," Jax high-fived Tristen.

Lydia stood up for her turn. As she passed Tristen, she

paused. "Good game," she said with a small smile.

Tristen looked surprised but pleased. "Thanks, you too."

Maddie beamed at the exchange. She knew it was Lydia's way of showing acceptance. Her best friend could be stubborn, but she had a good heart. Maddie loved her for it.

The group continued bowling into the evening, their laughter echoing through the alley. For a few precious hours, they were just normal teenagers having fun together. For once, Maddie kept her thoughts of Makenna at bay and just lived her life. That was a challenge all on its own, but it was one day where Maddie successfully lived without feeling the guilt that weighed her down for so long.

As they finally gathered their things to leave, Maddie felt lighter than she had in a long time. With her friends by her side, she had hope again. Hope that there could still be bright moments like this, even amidst the pain that lived in the recesses of her mind. That small light of hope was enough for Maddie to latch onto. She prayed it continued to lead her to a future where she could be free from the burdens she carried with her everywhere.

Chapter 17

Maddie stared at the blank canvas before her, brush poised but unmoving. The afternoon light filtering through the window of the art studio only seemed to mock her creative block. It was their last class of the day.

Maddie sighed, lowering her brush. If only it were that easy. Today, she was distracted by a sadness that had seemed to haunt her all day. It had all started when she woke up from her dream, a flashback of Makenna's funeral. Maddie had trouble shaking the images for the rest of the day. Every time she tried to put her brush down on the canvas, she just couldn't muster the energy to create. Each empty canvas only echoed the vast hollowness inside.

Tristen didn't seem to have the same block she did. His passion for art shone in his focused gaze and decisive strokes. He made it look effortless, probably because he cared more about art than he did throwing any move on the football field. His father would never understand that, though. Daniel Grant wanted Tristen to follow in his footsteps so badly he had stacked a mountain of expectations on his shoulders. And even with all that pressure, here Tristen stood, focused on the artwork in front of him.

She was slightly envious. Maddie yearned to

recapture that creative spark within herself. The last piece she had brought to life was over two weeks ago. She'd been preoccupied with balancing school with the secrets she kept from her family. It was becoming harder to manage. At home, Maddie found herself even more withdrawn than she had before, not that her parents seemed to notice. They were both so busy with their jobs that Maddie seemed to be more of a second thought most days.

Whenever things got really bad for Maddie, she would pop over to Grandma Minnie's and sit with her on her porch, sipping the ice tea that always seemed to cure her melancholy. Gran always said let's sip it out, Maddie girl. The two would talk about anything that came to mind. It was her safe place to talk about Makenna. Minnie was always ready to let Maddie talk about her sister, no matter what emotions it brought with it.

Glancing at Tristen's painting, an ache of longing pierced her heart. The bold colors and fluid forms expressed a lighter hope she feared lost forever. Yet Tristen's quiet encouragement rekindled a glimmer of hope. Perhaps one day, her own inner light would shine again, and she would learn to live in the moment instead of measuring every second against the guilt of outliving her sister.

Maddie put her brush to paper and recalled her sister's face, so like her own, but instead of seeing the end in her mind, Maddie searched for a time when life had been easier. She started to paint the curve of her face. For now, she contented herself observing this dedicated artist who saw beauty even in darkness. Witnessing the birth of Tristen's vision into the world gave Maddie the courage to keep going, to keep creating and living.

As she painted, the memories of her and Makenna as children flooded back. She remembered the countless times they had spent in their own makeshift studio, playing and painting together. It was where they had developed their love for art. Maddie smiled to herself as she continued to paint, feeling Makenna's presence with her in the room. The hollow echo that usually followed was a little lighter than usual, as if Maddie was given a brief pause from her grief. She was thankful for that moment.

Suddenly, Tristen's hand grabbed hers. His touch sent shivers down her spine, but Maddie ignored them, focusing instead on his words. "Your painting is beautiful," he whispered. "It looks just like her."

Maddie felt a warmth spreading through her body at his words. She had always been drawn to Tristen and his kind heart, even though their love was forbidden. Her father had made it clear that the Grant family was to be avoided at all costs, but Maddie had never been able to resist Tristen's charm. She dreamed of the day her father would get over his issues with Tristen's father. She found it odd that her father could forgive others so easily but couldn't look past the pain of his high school days, not even for her own happiness.

And Tristen did make her happy. Happier than she had been in the past few years. With him, she didn't feel the hole in her heart for a short time. He didn't make her forget Makenna, just made her loss a little easier to manage. She found love and acceptance with him. Maddie turned towards Tristen, finding herself lost in his gaze. The look in his eyes told her everything she needed to know; he felt the same way about her. If they had been alone instead of in a classroom with onlookers, they might have kissed, but this wasn't the time or place.

Tristen's hand lingered on hers for a moment longer before he withdrew it to continue his own painting. Maddie felt a pang of longing as she watched him work, her mind drifting to thoughts of what might have been if they weren't forbidden from being together. She pushed the thought aside and poured herself into her painting once again.

As the class drew to a close, Maddie stepped back to examine her work. It was a portrait of Makenna, and it was one of the best paintings she had ever done. It captured Makenna's spirit perfectly, the light in her eyes and the hope in her smile. For the first time since Makenna's passing, Maddie felt proud of herself and what she had created.

"Beautiful work, Maddie," Tristen said, coming up beside her. "She would have loved it."

Maddie looked over at him, grateful for his presence. "Thank you, Tristen," she said softly. "It means a lot coming from you."

Tristen smiled at her, and Maddie felt her heart skip a beat. She wanted nothing more than to take his hand and run out of the classroom with him, but she knew that wasn't an option.

"Same time tomorrow?" Tristen asked, breaking Maddie out of her daydream.

Maddie nodded, smiling at him. "I'll see you then."

As Tristen packed up his supplies and left the room, Maddie stood there for a moment longer, staring at her painting. She couldn't believe how much it resembled Makenna. It was like her sister was with her again, even if just in spirit. But as she packed up her own painting supplies, her mind drifted back to Tristen. The way his hand had felt in hers when he complimented her painting. The way his eyes seemed to look right through her as if he knew every hidden part of her soul.

Maddie knew she shouldn't be thinking about him like that. Her father would never approve, and it wasn't like they could just run away and be together. But the forbidden nature of their love only made it feel more intense, more real.

When she went home that night, she put her painting of Makenna on her desk. When her mother came in to say good night, her eyes were filled with tears when she saw it.

"Your sister would have loved this, Maddie," her mother whispered, her hand resting on Maddie's shoulder. "You have a gift for capturing the spirit of those you love."

Maddie smiled, feeling a small sense of pride at her mother's words. "Thank you, Mom."

As her mother left the room, Maddie sat down at her desk and reached for her phone. She hesitated for a moment before typing out a text to Tristen.

"Can't stop thinking about you," she wrote, biting her lip nervously as she hit send. It wasn't long before she received a reply.

"Same here. Wish we could be together," Tristen wrote back.

Maddie's heart raced as she read his words. Part of her wanted to give in to the temptation, to sneak out of the house and run away with him. But the rational part of her knew that wasn't possible. They continued to text back and forth for a while longer before Maddie finally forced herself to put the phone down and go to bed. As she lay there in the dark, she couldn't help but think about Tristen and what it would be like to be with him. She knew it was forbidden, but that only seemed to make it more exciting.

The next day, as Maddie made her way to art class, she couldn't shake the feeling of nervousness in her stomach. She knew being around Tristen would only make things harder for her, but she couldn't help herself. Guilt was starting to eat at her consciousness. For one, she was lying to her father, something she had never done before. Maddie had always told him the truth, even when the truth was the hardest thing to tell. She knew she was letting him down, and if he ever found out, he would never let her live it down. Maddie would probably be grounded for the rest of her life.

And while that guilt was heavy, there was another

one that held a crushing weight over her. Her thoughts often turned to her sister and how she would never know the joys of first love or the exhilaration of kissing a cute boy. There were so many life experiences Makenna would never have, and it wasn't fair.

Maddie closed her eyes and stopped just outside the art room and tried to shake the thoughts that threatened to tank her limited happiness. This had become her pattern throughout her day. Deal with the guilt, forgive herself for being the one to survive, and do her best to pull it all together so her life didn't completely fall to pieces. Joy was limited, but she was struggling to grasp it in her hands and hold on tight. Some days, she felt like she was white-knuckling it, she held on so hard.

Maddie took a deep breath, opened her eyes, and walked into the studio. The familiar smell of paint and turpentine washed over her the minute she stepped one foot inside it. After setting her things at her table, she went to retrieve the supplies she would need for the day. She carried a blank canvas tucked under one arm, brushes and palette in hand. Though she had not painted much since her sister's death, today, she felt inspired to try again.

She saw Tristen standing at his easel, focused intently on a seascape. Maddie felt a flutter in her stomach as she approached him, her heart racing with anticipation.

"Hey," she said softly, placing her bag down on the table next to his.

Tristen turned to her, a smile spreading across his face. "Hey, yourself. You ready to create some magic today?"

Maddie nodded eagerly, excitement coursing through her veins. She had been looking forward to this art class all day. As she began to unpack her supplies, Tristen moved closer to her, leaning in so close that Maddie could smell the subtle scent of his cologne.

"Your painting yesterday was amazing," he told her, his voice low and seductive. "I couldn't stop thinking about it all night."

Maddie felt heat rising to her cheeks as she met his gaze. "Thanks," she said softly, trying to quell the butterflies in her stomach.

"I'm almost done with my painting now." Tristen gestured to the painting before him.

Maddie came closer, gasping softly as the painting came into focus. The sunset ocean blazed with light, radiant beams shining through brooding clouds. She was transfixed by the motion of the waves, the way the paint danced and flowed across the canvas.

"Tristen, it's beautiful," she breathed. She admired the deft blend of colors, the life infused into each brushstroke. In the painting's light, she felt her own inner darkness receding, if only for a moment.

"Do you like it?" he asked, suddenly shy.

"I love it," Maddie replied. "The way you captured the light...it's so full of hope."

Tristen flushed with pride. "I'm glad. I was hoping it might inspire you."

"How could it not?" Maddie smiled up at him.

"I made this for you," he said. "I wanted you to have something beautiful, to remind you there's still light in the world."

Maddie's eyes filled with tears. Tristen had seen her pain and wanted to ease it, even for just a moment.

"You didn't have to do that," she said, voice thick with emotion.

"I know," Tristen replied gently. "But I wanted to."

A tear slipped down Maddie's cheek. Since her sister's death, kindness from others overwhelmed her. Tristen's gesture opened the floodgates.

Seeing her tears, Tristen stepped closer. "Hey, it's okay," he murmured.

Maddie shook her head, smiling through her tears. "Happy tears," she whispered.

Tristen carefully removed the canvas from the easel and handed it to her. Maddie held it close, letting the colors infuse her spirit.

"Thank you," she said softly. "I'll treasure this always."

Tristen squeezed her shoulder, smiling. The two artists stood together in the fading light, hearts full of inspiration and hope.

Maddie gazed at the painting, taking in every brushstroke and nuance of color. She could see how Tristen had layered the hues, starting with a fiery orange base and gradually shifting into cooler purples and blues towards the top. "I love how you captured the way the sunset fades. It's like I can feel the light disappearing."

Tristen nodded, pleased she had noticed. "That's exactly what I was going for. I used thicker paint in the foreground to make it feel more intense and energetic, then thinned it out as I worked upwards."

He pointed to a section of choppy brushstrokes in the water. "I also played around with texture here to give the illusion of waves and motion."

Maddie smiled, impressed by his technical skill. She could see how every choice he made, from composition to color, enhanced the overall mood of the piece. "You really are talented, Tristen."

Tristen flushed, touched by her words. "That means the world coming from you," he said. "You've helped me through a dark time too. I wanted to give you something to lift your spirits, too."

Maddie impulsively gave him a hug. "Mission accomplished," she said, beaming. The two artists stood back to admire the sunset scene, spirits soaring through art's redemptive power.

"Thank you," she whispered. "For seeing me...for understanding me...for this."

She gestured to the painting, then placed a hand tenderly on his cheek. Through misty eyes, she gazed at this boy who had come to mean so much.

Tristen's expression softened. He gently brushed a strand of hair from her face, tucking it behind her ear.

"You don't have to thank me," he said. "Spending time with you is a gift."

He paused as if considering his next words carefully. "You inspire me in a way no one else does. When I'm with you, I see the world differently...full of hope and beauty. I've fallen for you, Maddie."

"I've fallen for you too," she confessed. Looking around the classroom around her, she made sure no one else was listening to their conversation. Thankfully, everyone else was distracted with their own projects, even the teacher, who seemed more interested in whatever article she was reading on her phone. If no one was here, she would kiss him, but it wasn't safe to do so right now. His eyes displayed the same emotion.

Maddie cleared her throat. "We should probably get to work."

"Yeah. No fraternizing on school grounds," teased Tristen.

"And definitely not in the classroom where everyone can see." Maddie fought the urge to giggle like a little schoolgirl. Her heart was light as she picked up her brush and started to plan out her next art project.

Chapter 18

Tristen's gaze was heavy and empty, his eyes transfixed on the cereal bowl. The flakes swirled around in the milk, dissipating quickly as they sank into it, fading away until there was nothing left but a soggy mess.

"Eat up, son, you've got a big game tonight," his dad said, clapping a heavy hand on Tristen's shoulder.

Tristen winced, the weight feeling like a vise grip.

He shoved a spoonful of sweet, soggy cereal into his mouth. The cereal was the same as yesterday and the day before that. He did not taste it but chewed slowly on autopilot, staring at the empty bowl.

"Gotta get that protein in ya for the championship," his dad continued. "Those other boys won't know what hit 'em when you plow 'em down on that field."

Tristen swallowed hard, the lump of cereal sticking in his throat. He could already feel the other players' bones cracking under his crushing tackles and hear the crowd roar as he steamrolled to another touchdown. But the cheers always faded to echoes now, the lights dimming to a haze.

"You hear me, son?" His dad's voice boomed, snapping Tristen back. "Your head in the game tonight?"

"Yeah...sure, Dad," Tristen mumbled.

As he pushed away from the table, Maddie's face came to his mind. She was the only thought that had given him a semblance of peace in his life lately, but even that was forbidden. He couldn't help the way he felt for her, just like he couldn't help that his heart raced every time he saw her. Her image flashed by his eyes, reminding him of all he had to lose.

Tristen didn't know how long he stood there, lost in thought, until his dad's voice shook him back to reality. "You better be ready tonight, boy." The stern tone of his voice echoed with a threat because there was no second chance at victory.

Tristen nodded, swallowing hard to push down the knot of fear creeping up in his throat. He had to win tonight. It wasn't just about the game anymore; it was about proving himself. No matter what it takes.

He picked up his backpack and headed out the door, not looking back at the man who expected so much from him. The bitter taste of cereal still lingered in his mouth as he made his way to school. The sun had barely risen, casting a yellow-orange glow on everything in its path. There were few cars on the road, and he could hear the crunching of gravel beneath his sneakers as he walked across the parking lot.

At school, the hallways buzzed with Friday night energy. Players high-fived Tristen, and girls fluttered eyelashes and whispered excitedly. Under the bright fluorescent lights, he felt like he was sleepwalking through a strange, vivid dream.

"T-man! You ready to crush tonight?" A teammate hollered.

Tristen forced a smile. "Yeah, should be a good game," he said flatly. The thought of stepping on that field tonight made him feel like he was suffocating.

But he swallowed down the lump in his throat once more and walked on. Just one more game, he told himself. One more. And then there would be another and another.

There was always just one more.

Tristen shuffled to his locker, turning the combination lock with numb fingers. As the door creaked open, a flash of color caught his eye. He reached in and carefully pulled out a sketch — an expertly drawn portrait of himself in his football uniform, helmet under his arm, gazing thoughtfully into the distance.

Tristen's breath caught in his chest. No one had captured him like this before, seen past the tough jock exterior. He knew immediately it was Maddie's work. He could tell by the way she'd perfectly rendered the contours of his face, the depths of his eyes.

Footsteps approached down the hall. Tristen quickly folded the sketch and tucked it into his backpack just as Tiffany bounced up.

"So, we're all ready to cheer you on tonight," she said, popping her gum as she sashayed in her short cheer skirt. "And I was thinking we could maybe go out after, you know, celebrate?"

She smiled flirtatiously and placed a hand on Tristen's arm. He shifted away.

"We've already been over this, Tiffany. It's not going to happen," he mumbled, slamming his locker shut. "I gotta get to class."

Tiffany's face fell as Tristen turned and hurried off down the hall. But he didn't care — the only thing on his mind was finding Maddie, thanking her for the drawing. For seeing him, really seeing him, when no one else did.

Tristen was lost in thought as he made his way to first period, Maddie's sketch folded carefully in his backpack. He couldn't stop thinking about her talent, the way she had captured something deeper in him than his surface-level football persona. He pulled it out one more time to look at it as he walked down the hallway to his locker.

As he rounded the corner, raucous laughter echoed down the hall. Tristen looked up to see his teammates gathered around his locker. He didn't have time to put the sketch away before they could see it. One of them pulled the sketch from his hands.

"Well, well, lookie what we got here," jeered Brett, the quarterback. "Tristen's got himself a secret admirer!"

The other players whooped and hollered, tossing the sketch back and forth. Tristen's stomach dropped.

"Who's the chick that drew this sap?" scoffed Chad. "She must be blind or desperate."

More laughter. Tristen froze, unsure what to do. He wanted to grab the sketch back and tell them to stop, but he knew that would only invite more ridicule.

So he forced a laugh, trying to seem casual. "Yeah, crazy, right? Just some art chick with a crush."

Inside, his heart ached. He hated talking about Maddie like that, dismissing her work, which had meant so much. But he had to play it cool, pretend it was all a joke.

Tristen saw Maddie down the hall, her eyes wide as she watched the scene play out. He could see the hurt etched on her face as she realized what was happening. She had put herself out there, shown Tristen her true feelings, and now it was all being mocked. "Give it here," Tristen ordered.

"Hey, Maddie!" called Brett, waving the sketch in the air. "Is this your work?"

Maddie hesitated for a moment before nodding slowly. Her voice was barely above a whisper when she spoke, "Yeah, it is."

The players let out another round of jeering laughter, making crude comments about Tristen and Maddie's relationship. Tristen felt his fists clench at his sides as he watched them torment her.

The guys chortled, crumpling up the sketch and tossing

it in the trash. "You should stick to finger painting next time," Brett snickered.

Maddie marched straight toward Brett and the others, eyes blazing.

"Hey!" she shouted. "I want my sketch back."

The guys turned, smirking. "Oh yeah? Well, we trashed it, sweetheart. It wasn't even that good."

Tristen watched helplessly as Maddie's cheeks reddened.

"You had no right to take it," she said, voice wavering only slightly. "It wasn't for you."

"Aww, did we hurt your feelings?" Chad sneered. "We were just having a little fun."

He grabbed a marker from his backpack and scrawled crude drawings across the page. "Here, I fixed it for you."

The other players guffawed. Maddie's eyes glistened as she snatched back the defaced page.

"You guys are jerks," she whispered.

She crumpled the paper, and as it slipped from her fingers, she fled down the hall. Tristen ached to run after her, to comfort her and apologize. But he remained frozen, hating himself for his silence, for caring too much what the others thought. Maddie deserved so much better. And he had failed her.

Tristen watched Maddie's face turn pale before she headed in the other direction. Tristen felt powerless. The other boys sauntered off, leaving Tristen standing there, fuming silently. He picked the sketch up from the floor and carefully folded it back up to stash in his backpack. He didn't care that they had defaced it. It was still beautiful to him.

The day dragged on in a blur of lectures and notes, but all Tristen could think about was the sketch in his backpack and Maddie's reaction to the teasing. He knew he needed to speak to her about what had happened.

After the bell for their last class rang, Tristen waited a few minutes before making his way to the art classroom. When he arrived, she was already working on her project with a dead focus that told him she wasn't ready to talk. He spent the rest of class working quietly by her side.

At last, the final bell rang. Tristen lingered by his locker, watching students stream toward the exit. He hoped to catch a glimpse of Maddie to gauge if she was okay. But there was no sign of her in the sea of teenagers. With a sigh, Tristen shoved his books into his bag and headed out to the student parking lot. As he approached his dusty pickup, he spotted a familiar figure perched on the tailgate.

Maddie.

She looked up as he drew nearer, uncertainty etched across her delicate features. Tristen's heart leapt at the sight of her. But the memory of her crumpled, defeated expression that morning tempered his joy.

"Hey," he said softly.

"Hey."

An awkward beat of silence. Tristen set his bag down and leaned against the truck beside her.

"Listen, Maddie..." He hesitated, searching for the right words. "About today, I'm really sorry. I should've stood up for you. I was a coward."

She nodded, lips pressed in a thin line. "It's okay. I get why you didn't say anything."

"No, it's not okay," Tristen said firmly. "You deserve better than that. Better than me."

Maddie turned to face him. The late afternoon sun illuminated her eyes, still rimmed red from crying.

"I don't want better, Tristen," she said softly. "I want you."

Tristen's heart swelled. He reached for her hand, intertwining their fingers.

"I want you too," he whispered. "I'll make this right, I promise."

Maddie offered a small, tentative smile. There was still hurt there and uncertainty about what would come next. But also hope. Tristen knew the path forward would be difficult. But with Maddie by his side, he was ready to face it.

Chapter 19

As she closed the door to her room behind her, she couldn't help but wonder what the future held for her and Tristen. Would they ever be able to be together? There had to be a day for them somewhere in the future where none of these boundaries were glaring in their faces. Maddie was just hoping she could hold out until then.

Maddie's shoulders tensed when she heard the front door slam shut downstairs. She kept her eyes glued to her English homework, though the words blurred together on the page. Maddie's heart raced as she heard her father's booming voice calling her name from the bottom of the stairs.

"Maddie!" Her father's voice boomed through the house once more. "Get down here!"

She took a deep breath before closing her textbook. As she descended the stairs, she caught a glimpse of her father's scowl. His arms were crossed, his eyebrows knitted together. Her father's eyes were narrowed as he glared at her, his arms crossed over his chest. Maddie could almost feel the heat emanating from his body.

"Where were you last night?" he demanded. Before she could respond, he continued. "I called Lydia's mom. You weren't there."

Maddie swallowed hard. She had spent the evening with Tristen, watching the sunset at the park. His smile flashed through her mind, the way his hand felt clasped in hers.

"I was just driving around with some friends," she said quietly. It wasn't completely a lie.

Her father stepped closer, eyes flashing. "Do you know how dangerous that is? Just driving around with God knows who?" His voice grew louder. "Ever since your sister —" He stopped himself short, pain creasing his face.

Maddie's throat tightened at the mention of Makenna. She knew her father blamed himself, wishing he could've protected his little girl from the cancer that stole her away. His overprotectiveness of Maddie had only grown since they lost her twin.

"I'm sorry, Dad," Maddie said gently. "I should've told you where I was."

He sighed, features softening. "I just need to know you're safe." He pulled her into a hug. She clung to him, wishing she could stay in the safety of his arms instead of venturing into the uncertainty of first love.

Robert held Maddie tight, then pulled back to look at her. "Who were these friends you were with?"

Maddie hesitated. She knew her father was wary of anyone he didn't know well. "Just some kids from school."

Robert's eyes narrowed. "Which kids?"

"My friends." Maddie avoided his eye contact. She knew this wasn't going to go down well.

"Don't lie to me, Maddie. What is this I hear about you sneaking around with Tristen Grant?" he growled, his voice low and dangerous.

Maddie felt a lump form in her throat as she tried to come up with a response. She knew that anything she said would only make it worse. It was time to face the music.

"I...I don't know what you're talking about," she stammered, knowing that her words sounded weak even to her own ears.

"Don't lie to me, Maddie," he spat out her name like it was poison on his tongue. "One of the cheerleaders saw you with him at the park last week."

Maddie felt anger flare inside of her. Tiffany! That rat! She had no right to be spreading rumors about her and Tristen. For her to tell her father was lower than low. They had done nothing wrong, and yet they were constantly being punished for their fathers' rivalry.

"Why does it matter who I'm with?" she asked, feeling a sense of rebellion rising within her. "It's not like we're doing anything wrong."

Her father's face turned red with anger as he stepped closer to her. "If you think I'm going to stand by while my daughter gets involved with Daniel Grant's son, then you've got another thing coming." His voice was now a menacing whisper.

Maddie stood her ground, her eyes blazing with defiance. "Tristen is not our enemy, Dad. He's just a guy that I happen to like."

Her father's nostrils flared as he took a step closer to her. "He's the son of the man who ruined my life," he spat out. "And I'll be damned if I let you have anything to do with him."

There was a dangerous gleam in his eyes that Maddie had never seen before. She could feel the tension between them rising by the second. She knew she had to tread carefully, or things would spiral out of control.

"Dad, please," she said, her voice now soft and pleading. "I know that things have been bad between our families for a long time, but that doesn't mean that Tristen and I can't be friends. We have the same classes, we have study groups together. We're in the same youth group at Church. You can't mean for me to ignore him completely. I won't do it."

Her father looked at her for a long moment before

letting out a deep sigh. "Fine," he said, his voice now calm but still tinged with anger. "You can be friends with him. But that's all it can ever be."

Maddie felt a sense of relief wash over her as she nodded her head in agreement. She knew it wasn't ideal, but it was better than nothing. She turned and walked up the stairs, feeling her heart still racing with adrenaline.

Maddie lay on her bed, tears flowing down her cheeks. She felt utterly helpless and frustrated. Her father didn't understand. He didn't know how she felt when she was with Tristen. How could he forbid her from seeing the one person who made her feel alive again?

She heard a soft knock on her door. "Go away," she said thickly, wiping at her eyes.

The door opened, and her father came in, his face solemn. "Maddie, we need to talk."

Maddie sat up, glaring at him. "I don't want to talk to you."

Robert sighed. "I know you're upset, but try to understand. I just want to protect you."

"From what?" Maddie cried. "Tristen would never hurt me!"

"Maybe not intentionally," Robert said. "But that family is dangerous. If you only knew how his father..."

"Tristen isn't like him!" Maddie insisted.

Robert shook his head. "I'm sorry, but my decision is final. You are not to see that boy anymore outside of school or church." His voice was stern.

Maddie leapt to her feet. "You can't do this! You can't control my life!"

"As long as you live under my roof, you'll follow my rules," Robert said firmly.

"So I'm just your prisoner now?" Maddie felt like she'd been slapped. She choked back a sob.

Robert reached out to her, but she recoiled from his touch. "Please try to understand."

But Maddie had enough. She fled past him, down the stairs and out the front door, blinded by tears. She had to get away, clear her head, and figure out what to do next. But deep down, she feared her father's stubbornness meant she might never see Tristen again. The thought was too much to bear. Maddie rushed into the garage, slamming the side door behind her. The small, cluttered space was her sanctuary, the one place she could truly be alone. She flipped on the fluorescent lights, which flickered and hummed.

In the corner sat her easel, paint tubes and brushes scattered across a table next to it. Art was Maddie's escape, especially lately. Since Makenna had gotten sick, she'd spent hours working through her emotions on canvas. Lately, her works had been lighter, but today, she wasn't feeling like sunshine and daisies.

Maddie clenched her jaw, fighting back tears as she squeezed dollops of paint onto her palette. The colors swirled together, deep purple bleeding into crimson red. With broad, furious strokes, she began attacking the blank canvas. The garage was silent except for the scrape of bristles against fabric.

Maddie became absorbed in bringing the image in her mind to life on the canvas. With broad strokes of midnight blue, she depicted a night sky dotted with stars. Crimson streaks crossed the canvas as she added the silhouette of a girl reaching a hand up toward the heavens.

As she worked, Maddie's swirling emotions gradually calmed. The familiar motions of painting allowed her mind to process everything that had happened with her dad and Tristen. She knew her father only wanted to protect her, but she wished he could understand how she felt about Tristen.

The sound of the side door creaking open jolted Maddie

from her thoughts. She turned to see her mother come into the garage.

"Hey," Mom said softly, walking over to peek at Maddie's painting. "That's really good. What's it about?"

Maddie sighed, rinsing her brush in a cup of water. "Just...stuff with Dad. And Tristen."

Her mother nodded knowingly. She hopped up on a stool near Maddie's easel. "Wanna talk about it?"

Maddie hesitated. Part of her wanted to confide in her mom, but another part wanted to keep her feelings private. Besides, it wasn't like her mom had stood up for her at all. Instead, she'd let her dad go on his rampage about the Grant family and tear down any hope Maddie had for a normal future.

"I don't know," Maddie finally said. "Dad's being so unreasonable. He won't even give Tristen a chance."

Her mom gave her a sympathetic look. "He's just worried about you. But maybe he'll come around eventually."

Maddie sighed again. It was nice to hear that her mom was on her side, even if she didn't quite vocalize it to her father just yet. Maddie wasn't sure she wanted her parents fighting over her, though. They were barely hanging on after losing Makenna. "I hope so." She picked up her brush, dipping it in a puddle of orange paint. There was still more work to be done.

"I know he seems strict," Mom continued gently. "But Dad loves you. He just wants to keep you safe."

Maddie's brush hovered over the canvas. She blinked back tears that suddenly stung her eyes. Why did Maddie have to be the one to consider everyone else's feelings all the time? Why did that have to be her burden to bear?

"I know," she said thickly. "But he doesn't get it. Tristen's not like what Dad thinks. He would never hurt me."

Mom was quiet for a moment. In the background, the

old garage fridge hummed softly.

"Have you told Dad that?" Her mother finally asked. "About who Tristen really is?"

Maddie shook her head, a tear slipping down her cheek. "I tried, but he wouldn't listen. He's already made up his mind."

She thought about Tristen's kind eyes and his warm laugh. The way he looked at her like she was the only person in the world. If her dad would just give him a chance, then maybe he would see the good in him, too.

"Maybe you could help change his mind," Mom suggested gently. "I could talk to him, too, if you want."

Maddie looked up, feeling a swell of gratitude for her mother. She managed a small smile. "Thanks, Mom. I doubt it will help, though. He's pretty set in his ways."

"Well, I'll leave you to it." Mom gave her a soft hug before leaving the garage.

Maddie's anger was more diffused now. She went back to her canvas and continued painting. Gradually, the colors started blending together like they were meant to be, just like Tristen and Maddie. Maybe it was time for her to stand up for herself and tell her dad how she felt about Tristen. It was a risk, but so was loving him in secret. Her heart raced with the thought of confronting her father, but she knew she had to try.

With renewed resolution, Maddie picked up her brush and started painting again. Each stroke carried with it a sense of strength and determination, a reflection of what Maddie was feeling deep inside. She lost track of time as she painted, only stopping when the garage was bathed in complete darkness.

Maddie headed back into the house, feeling exhausted but also strangely elated. She felt like she had gained some sort of clarity from painting as if the images on the canvas were a physical manifestation of the emotions she had been bottling up inside.

Chapter 20

Tristen gazed out the rain-streaked window of his bedroom, watching the droplets race down the glass. He should be happy. At the end of the year, he'd graduate high school and head off to college. If only his father didn't expect him to play football wherever he chose. His father's path for him was football and a bachelor of science in business. Daniel Grant had never made it to college football, instead choosing to work a job at the local car lot. He had moved his way up over the years and was now the owner of the biggest dealership in the Mellow Creek area, with lots in the next three cities that he micromanaged.

Tristen could not imagine spending his life convincing someone else to sign their life away on the dotted line. He wasn't sure what he wanted to be or if he should know the answer to that right now. All he knew was that he wanted to be able to continue doing his art and that this part of him was something his father would never relate to.

Maddie and Tristen had talked about where they might want to go to school, but Maddie was a year behind him. Wherever he went, Maddie promised to follow. He knew he couldn't hold her to that, but his heart hoped that were true. He knew her better than anyone else. Not once did Maddie look down on him for not being the hard-hitting macho football player that everyone expected him to be. He had tender edges, ones he had never felt safe sharing with anyone else.

There was a sharp rap at his bedroom door.

"Dinner's ready," his father called gruffly from the hallway.

Tristen sighed. "Yeah. I'll be right down."

At the dining room table, Tristen picked at his food, hyperaware of his father's scrutinizing gaze. The clink of silverware on china plates echoed in the cavernous room.

Finally, Daniel broke the tense silence. "So, Tristen, have you given more thought to which college recruits you're looking for?"

"Again?" Lily Grant sighed as she prepared to listen to another conversation that would probably not go well.

Tristen shook his head. "I really like ASU. They have a great business department, and I could minor in art."

Daniel's face hardened. "Art? I thought that was just a hobby. Well, I won't have a son of mine wasting his time scribbling when he should be preparing for his future." He took a bite of steak, chewing slowly before fixing Tristen with a stern look.

"And I don't want you spending so much time with that girl either. It's bad enough I got to deal with Coach Tyler from the sidelines. You don't need to fraternize with the enemy."

Tristen gripped his fork tightly, anger flaring in his chest. "The enemy? Coach Tyler is a pretty good coach. I like him."

"Well, if you knew him the way I did." Daniel shoved some of the food on his plate around with his fork.

"What do you want me to do, ignore her? We go to the same church and the same school and belong to the same youth group. We're bound to run into each other."

Tristen only felt a small nibble of guilt. Only a small

portion of what he was saying was the truth. Maddie wasn't just someone he would run into. She was someone he would run to every day of the week. Maddie was like oxygen when all the air around him was sucked dry.

"From what I heard, you're doing more than running into her, Tristen. I have eyes and ears everywhere. I don't want you to see that girl. She's bad news." His father's chest puffed out like he was putting his foot down, and there would be no arguing.

"Daniel," his mother tried to interrupt, but her words were not noticed.

"You don't know anything about her." Tristen clenched his fork tight in his hand, prepared to fight for the girl he loved.

Daniel slammed his fist on the table, making the dishes rattle. "If you continue to see her, you can kiss your college money goodbye. You'll need a lot more than a football scholarship to pay your way, Tristen. I won't pay for you to ruin your life."

Tristen met his father's icy stare, heart pounding. He had to choose: Maddie or his future. The decision was impossible, but he had to find a way. Tristen pushed back his chair and stood up abruptly.

"I'm not hungry anymore," he muttered before turning and rushing upstairs to his bedroom.

Once inside, he locked the door and leaned against it, taking deep breaths to calm his racing heart. His father's threat echoed in his mind. How could he choose between Maddie and his dreams for the future? She was his muse, his inspiration. When he was with her, he felt truly alive and free to be himself.

Crossing the room, Tristen knelt beside his bed and pulled out a large sketchpad from underneath. He leafed through page after page of drawings of Maddie — her eyes, her lips, the curve of her cheek. In charcoal and pencil, he had captured her beauty, her spirit, her warmth.

Drawing centered him and allowed him to process his emotions. He began a new sketch, using swift, bold strokes to outline Maddie's face. As her image took form, the tightness in his chest eased slightly. With art as his outlet, perhaps he could find a way through this impasse with his father. He had to believe that somehow, love would find a way.

Tristen continued drawing late into the night, finding solace in his art. He would deal with his father and the choice ahead in the morning. For now, his love for Maddie flowed through his fingers onto the page. As long as he could draw her, he wasn't lost.

Tristen lost himself in his art, sketching furiously to capture the flood of emotions swirling within. Page after page, he poured his heartache onto the paper — Maddie's eyes brimming with tears, their hands desperately reaching for one another, his father looming over them like a storm cloud.

No matter how vividly Tristen drew, he couldn't escape the impossible decision before him. Stay with Maddie and lose his future, or leave her behind and live the life his father planned? Anguish tore through him at the thought of being without his muse, his love.

In a fit of despair, Tristen flung his sketchpad across the room. It hit the wall with a loud thud, loose pages scattering everywhere. He dropped his head into his hands, choking back sobs.

A gentle knock on the door broke the silence. "Tristen?" his mother's voice, soft and worried. "Please let me in."

Tristen steadied his breathing, then crossed over to open the door. His mother's kind eyes searched his face. Without a word, she stepped forward and folded him into her arms. Tristen clung to her, taking comfort in her embrace as the tears finally fell.

Tristen's mother held him for a long moment, letting him cry into her shoulder. When his sobs quieted to sniffles, she led him over to sit on the edge of his bed.

"I know how much she means to you," she said gently.

Tristen nodded, staring down at the floor. "I love her, Mom."

"I know, sweetheart." She brushed a hand through his hair. "Your father just wants what's best for you, even if he doesn't always show it well."

Tristen huffed bitterly. "Best for me or best for him?"

His mother sighed. "He's scared of losing you. Your art...it's your passion, but it won't pay the bills or put you through college. He doesn't mean to hurt you, Tristen. He just doesn't understand."

"So, I should just give up everything for him? Forget about Maddie and let him control my life?" Tristen's voice rose in anger.

"No one can choose your path but you," his mother said. "Maybe try talking to your father again when things have calmed down. Help him see how much your art means, how much Maddie means."

Tristen looked up, a flicker of hope in his eyes. "You really think he'll listen?"

She squeezed his hand. "Just speak from your heart. He loves you, Tristen. The rest will work itself out."

Tristen felt the weight on his chest lift slightly. As long as he had his mother on his side, he could get through this. He stood and crossed to the blank canvas propped against the wall. Picking up a pencil, he began lightly sketching the outline of a face.

Maddie's face. No matter what happened, he would find a way back to her.

Tristen stared at the sketch, thinking of Maddie's warm

brown eyes and radiant smile. How could his father expect him to just walk away from the girl who made him feel truly alive for the first time?

Sighing, he set down the pencil and pulled out his phone. His finger hovered over Maddie's number, hesitating. Ever since his father's ultimatum at dinner two nights ago, a tense awkwardness had crept into their interactions. Maddie could tell something was weighing on him, but Tristen couldn't bring himself to tell her about his father's threats. He didn't want to drag her into this mess or make her feel responsible for coming between him and his family.

Taking a deep breath, Tristen hit call. After three rings, Maddie's melodic voice came through. "Hey, you," she said softly.

"Hey," Tristen replied, suddenly unsure what to say.

An uneasy silence stretched between them. Finally, Maddie spoke again, her voice tinged with concern. "Tristen, what's going on? You've been acting so distant the past couple of days. Did...did I do something wrong?"

"No!" Tristen cut in hurriedly. "No, you didn't do anything wrong. It's me, I just..." He trailed off with a frustrated sigh.

"Talk to me," Maddie pleaded. "Let me in, Tristen. I'm here for you, no matter what."

Tristen blinked back sudden tears, overwhelmed by her steadfast loyalty and love. He had to tell her the truth. "It's my dad," he began hesitantly. "He found out about us, and he's not happy. He gave me an ultimatum — end things with you, or he'll stop paying for college."

Maddie gasped softly. "Oh Tristen, I'm so sorry. What are you going to do?"

"I don't know," he admitted. "I can't lose you, Maddie. But I can't throw away my future either. I feel so lost and conflicted. I just wish I could find a way for us to be together without my dad's disapproval hanging over us."

"We'll figure it out," Maddie said, determination in her voice. "I believe in us, Tristen. No matter what your dad says or does, he can't change how we feel about each other. Our dads can't rule over us forever."

Tristen let her words wash over him, taking comfort in her resolve. As long as they faced this together, he knew they could make it through the storm.

Chapter 21

It was a bright Saturday morning. Maddie had spent the night with Grandma Minnie and was spending the early part of the morning helping her in the kitchen. As Maddie mixed the batter for the pancakes, her mind wandered to Tristen. They had been sneaking around, trying to keep their love a secret from everyone, but it was getting harder and harder. Maddie's father, who was also Tristen's coach, didn't treat him any different than the other players, but sometimes there was a glance that was off putting. Maddie had seen him do it and knew it must weigh on Tristen. Not only that, Tristen's father had also thrown his opinions into the mix.

Why did their dads have to hold a grudge? People can change? Why did they refuse to? Maybe Daniel Grant wasn't the same man he was years ago. Maddie was sure her father was still in that overprotective phase. He wanted to protect her from some unseen danger, probably because he couldn't protect Makenna from her cancer. Maddie loved her father, but Maddie couldn't help how she felt about Tristen. She didn't want to rebel against her dad. That had never been her intent. She simply knew what she wanted and was willing to fight for it.

"Hey there, sugar," Grandma Minnie said, grabbing Maddie's attention.

Maddie turned to her with a smile. "Hey, Grandma."

"You look a little distracted," Grandma Minnie said with a knowing look.

Maddie blushed. If Grandma Minnie could actually read her mind, she'd be in big trouble. "It's nothing."

Grandma Minnie chuckled. "Love is never nothing."

Maddie sighed, realizing that her grandma knew her better than anyone else on the face of the Earth. "I love him, Grandma. But my father —"

"I know, I know," Grandma Minnie interrupted. "Your father has some old grudges with his family. But you can't help who you love."

Maddie smiled gratefully at her grandmother. "Thank you for understanding."

Grandma Minnie patted her hand. "Always, my dear. One day, he might come around. Until then, you have to toe the line, Maddie."

"I know," mumbled Maddie.

As they continued making breakfast together, Maddie couldn't shake off the feeling that Makenna was there with them in spirit. She missed her twin so much; they used to do everything together. Even though Maddie was doing her best to get on with her life, there was still a constant reminder that her other half was absent.

After breakfast was ready and they sat down to eat, Maddie brought up Makenna. "Do you think she's watching over us?"

Grandma Minnie nodded solemnly. "Of course she is, baby girl."

"They never talk about her anymore." Maddie looked down at her plate.

"They're in pain, Maddie. Sometimes ignoring the pain makes it easier to live."

"But they're not really living. They barely talk to each other. Sometimes, I doubt they realize I'm alive. You're really the only one I can talk to. You don't erase her." Maddie moved her pancakes around through the syrup.

"I never could. You both are important to me." Grandma Minnie smiled at her, and her eyes carried a sorrow that Maddie related to. "Do you remember when you both rescued the nest of bunnies?"

"The neighbor's dog had tried to get into it." Maddie smiled.

"You and Makenna took turns guarding the nest around the clock. Almost scared the mother off, but you learned how to be patient and back off enough to make it safe for her to come back."

"Makenna refused to come inside that night. She slept on the porch, worried that some other critter would come along and attack them." Maddie remembered that night all too well.

"And then, when she was afraid, you snuck out to stay by her side. You two were always inseparable." Grandma Minnie recalled. "It must be hard to be without her."

A tear clouded Maddie's eyes. "It is. Just when I think I can't cry anymore and that there's light at the end of the tunnel, a new tidal wave hits me, and I remember every second I've been without her."

"That is grief and loss, Maddie. It's okay to feel it. You may feel it forever, but it will get better."

"My friends help. They let me talk about Makenna. They listen. I don't have to worry about upsetting them with her memory."

"Well, it's good that you're spending time with them today then." Grandma Minnie reached out to touch her hand. "It will do your heart good."

"Who's going to help you?" asked Maddie with concern.

"You do, Maddie. You do." Her grandma smiled at her

and squeezed her hand. "More than you could ever know."

At that moment, Maddie's phone dinged. She looked down to see that Lydia was already waiting outside. "Speaking of my friends. They're here. I'll just put these in the sink..."

"Don't you worry about those. I'll get them. Go have some fun, Maddie."

"Okay, Grandma. I love you."

"I love you too, child."

Maddie stood up and pushed her chair into the table. Turning around, she walked from the kitchen and made her way outside. She found Jax and Thomas had left her the front seat and almost did a small fist pump. Shotgun was always the best seat in the house. The day was starting to look up.

"Hey guys!" Maddie greeted them as she opened the car door.

"Someone's had coffee," accused Thomas.

"What?" asked Maddie innocently. Maybe she was pretending to be more chipper than she felt. Maybe it was the fact that she was planning to meet up with Tristen when they made it to their destination.

"Oh, leave her alone. Just cause you're not Suzie Sunshine," muttered Jax.

Lydia rolled her eyes. "They've been at it since I picked them up. I have a feeling it's going to be a *great* day."

"Maybe they just need to stretch their legs for a bit," suggested Maddie.

"They can do that when we get there." Lydia put the car in drive, and they took off.

Today, the four of them were heading to the nature preserve, where they would meet Tristen. As they drove down the road, Maddie couldn't help but feel a nervous excitement bubbling up inside of her. She stole a glance back at Jax and Thomas, who had switched gears from complaining mode and were now chatting excitedly about the day ahead.

As they pulled into the nature preserve's parking lot, Maddie spotted Tristen leaning against his truck, looking every bit as handsome and rugged as she remembered. Her heart skipped a beat as he approached the car. She took a deep breath and stepped out, trying to steady herself.

"Hey," he said with a smile, his eyes lighting up as he saw her.

"Hi," she replied softly, feeling a blush rise to her cheeks.

"Well, love birds, we're going to keep walking this way." Lydia pointed to the trail ahead.

"We may hang back for a few." Maddie was looking forward to just a little bit of time.

"We figured. Just don't stay too far behind," teased Jax.

As soon as the others disappeared from view, she moved closer to Tristen. His eyes lingered on her for a moment before he leaned in and brushed his lips against hers. Maddie's heart skipped a beat as she lost herself. It was a fleeting moment, all they really got these days with all the hoops they had to jump through to be together.

They pulled away, and Tristen took her hand as they walked towards the nature trails. Maddie felt the sun on her skin and the breeze in her hair as they strolled along. She was alive again, feeling like everything was right in the world. Maddie was determined to keep all the negative thoughts at bay.

Footsteps crunched on the path, and Maddie pulled away to see Lydia, Jax, and Thomas approaching. They must have taken the loop and turned around. Maddie smiled and waved. "Fancy meeting you again."

Lydia reached them first, eyebrows raised. "Well, we tried to give you enough time, but the trail is only so long, you know."

"Sorry we took so long," Tristen apologized.

Jax clapped a hand on Tristen's shoulder. "No judgment, man. We get it."

Thomas nodded, eyes gentle behind his glasses. "Your secret's safe with us."

Maddie let out a breath. "So, you guys are okay with this?"

"Of course," Lydia said. "We just want you to be happy. I always loved Romeo and Juliet."

"Me too, but this one better not end in tragedy," warned Jax.

"No way." Maddie waved off their words. "I've had enough of that to last me a lifetime."

Maddie's eyes stung with tears she refused to shed. She'd already shed enough today. Now was not the time. Now, she should be enjoying the limited time she had with Tristen and her friends. The sadness could encroach on her time and space later when she was alone in her room.

"Glad to hear it," added Lydia, who looked at her with concern. Her eyes sent a questioning glance to Maddie, for Lydia had come to read all of Maddie's emotional cues.

"Come on, let's get to our spot before the sun gets too high," Maddie said, eager to move on to lighter conversation. Besides, changing the topic would keep Lydia from asking any further questions.

The group hiked down the shaded trail that wound through the preserve, the trees dense enough to block out the morning heat. A family of deer watched them curiously before bounding into the underbrush. Birds sang their songs back and forth without a care in the world.

When they reached the meadow, Lydia spun in a slow circle, arms outstretched. "I can't get over how beautiful it is here."

Wildflowers carpeted the ground in purples, yellows, and whites. Birdsong filled the air as they unpacked the picnic basket. Maddie spread out a blanket, and they sat down, passing around sandwiches and fruit. The tart lemonade was refreshing after their hike.

As the three sat down on an outcropping of rocks to eat their packed lunch, Maddie told them the story her great-grandma used to tell about hidden treasure in the preserve's caverns. No one had ever found it, but the legend persisted. When people stopped visiting, and the park path was removed, and then trees grew over it, the family lost interest in finding what they thought was a fairy tale.

Tristen watched Maddie as she told the story, captivated by the way her expression changed with each detail. He had always loved how passionate she was about their family history and traditions. It was one of the many things that made him fall even harder for her.

"Can you show us where the cave is?" Thomas asked, his eyes sparkling with excitement.

Maddie looked hesitant. "I don't know if it's safe to go into the caves. They're off-limits to visitors, probably overridden. I'm not even sure if they're marked."

"But we won't tell anyone," Jax added with a grin.

Lydia rolled her eyes. "Guys, we shouldn't be encouraging breaking rules."

Tristen chuckled. "Relax, Lydia, we're not going to do anything crazy. We just want to see where it is."

Maddie finally conceded. "Alright, but I'm not promising anything."

They followed Maddie up the small hill to an overgrown path choked with weeds and bushes. After pushing through tangled branches and sharp thorns, they arrived at a large boulder blocking the entrance to a cave. Its mouth opened wide like gaping jaws awaiting their exploration; however, it was too dark inside for them to see anything beyond what was illuminated from the outside. A gust of stale air washed out of its depths — the smell reminding her of old books left unopened for too long in her grandmother's attic.

"We should probably leave now," Tristen said softly yet firmly in order to make sure that everyone heard him clearly despite the background noises around them.

"Yeah," agreed Jax reluctantly as his eyes swept across the imposing opening before him one more time, looking disappointed and curious all at once. "I guess this is our cue. Let's mark down where this place is so we can come back better prepared next time."

Lydia grabbed some twigs lying nearby and used them to move bushes aside while adding new sticks below to start marking the space. Gathering strength, she pulled a few flat rocks together before placing smooth, hand-sized ones above rough edges, creating makeshift markers that she and the others could follow in the future.

"I guess this is a good spot to turn around for now," said Maddie as they made their way back down the hill, each of them deep in thought over what lay beyond that entrance — not to mention stories of fantasizing about hidden treasures inside it. Throughout the remainder of the day, they discussed theory on various ways of how the caverns might be accessed properly, but ultimately, all agreed more research was needed before making any further attempts at exploring unsafe yet mysterious depths.

"Imagine what you'd do if you found a treasure chest full of gold and jewels," Maddie said wistfully. In her mind, she pictured a new life with Tristen, far from this town full of painful memories.

Jax grinned. "I'd buy a monster truck!"

Tristen moved closer to Maddie on the blanket, their shoulders touching. "I'd use that treasure to take you away from here," he said softly. "We could start over somewhere new, just the two of us."

Maddie's heart fluttered. She imagined driving off into the sunset with Tristen, the windows down and music blasting. No more pitying looks when people realized she was Makenna's twin. No more her dad's worried glances when he thought she couldn't see.

"I'd go anywhere with you," Maddie said. She pictured busy city streets full of strangers who had no idea who she was or what she'd lost. Maybe the treasure was just a legend. But she had found something real with Tristen. A chance to start again.

Maddie's reverie was broken by Lydia's voice. "Earth to Maddie! A little help?"

Maddie looked over to see Lydia and Jax struggling with the picnic basket while Thomas laughed. She jumped up to help them spread out the extra blanket and unpack the sandwiches and snacks.

"Sorry, I was daydreaming," Maddie said.

"Daydreaming about lover boy over there?" Lydia teased.

Maddie felt her face grow warm as she glanced at Tristen. He just grinned and shook his head.

"Leave her alone," Jax said, lightly shoving Lydia's shoulder. "It's nice to see Maddie happy for once."

"Yeah, we're just messing with you," Lydia said. "I think it's romantic."

Maddie smiled gratefully at her friends. She hadn't been sure how they would react to her seeing Tristen, but their support meant everything. Maddie was lucky to have such understanding friends.

Thomas flopped down on the blanket. "Can we eat now? I'm starving!"

Everyone laughed and joined him, passing around sandwiches and fruit. Maddie bit into a juicy peach, the sweetness bursting over her tongue. She watched a pair of swallowtail butterflies dance among the wildflowers. For the first time in a long while, her heart felt light.

Maddie leaned back on her hands, looking up at the wispy clouds drifting across the blue sky. She tried to imagine what it would be like to leave this place with Tristen. To start a whole new life somewhere far away.

Part of her felt guilty for even thinking about it. Her dad had already lost so much. But Maddie needed something for herself — a chance to move forward.

Tristen reached over and gave her hand a gentle squeeze. "You okay?" he asked softly.

Maddie nodded, intertwining her fingers with his. "Just thinking."

"Anything you want to share with the class?" Jax asked.

"Come on, spill," Lydia said.

Maddie took a deep breath. "I was just imagining what it would be like if Tristen and I left together. Started fresh somewhere new."

Her friends were silent for a moment.

"Wow," Thomas finally said. "That would be..."

"Epic," Jax finished with a grin.

Maddie looked at them in surprise. "So, you don't think it's crazy?"

"Maybe a little, but I don't blame you," Lydia said. "You two totally should do it, but maybe after you graduate next year? A girl's gotta have a diploma these days, after all."

"You're probably right. A girl can dream, though." Maddie smiled, buoyed by her friends' support. She glanced at Tristen, who looked thoughtful.

"Who knows what the future will bring," Tristen said.

Maddie's heart quickened. With her friends and Tristen at her side, anything seemed possible. The future felt bright with hope.

Chapter 22

The golden glow of the streetlamp illuminated Maddie's face as she sat alone on the weathered park bench. She shivered against the cold night air, her breath forming wispy clouds. The screech of crickets and the rustle of leaves filled the darkness.

Maddie had been waiting for her chance to sneak out and meet up with Tristen again. She recalled their first summer together, how it felt like they were untouchable, the thought of a future not even on their radar. But things had become infinitely more complicated with their parents. The only way they could see each other was to sneak around, and it was weighing on each of them.

Tonight, however, offered Maddie an unexpected window of opportunity: Her dad had to be away for business till late Saturday, and her mom had decided to take a break and go with him. It had been forever since Mom had gone on a business trip with Dad or a trip of any kind. Maddie was happy for her but happier for herself because that meant she got to spend time with Grandma Minnie, who not only went to bed early but gave her more freedom than her parents ever did.

Part of Maddie felt guilty for taking advantage of her grandma's good graces, but she couldn't seem to help herself. It was like she had stuck one toe into waters churning with defiance, and now her entire body was drenched with it. Her parents hadn't raised her to be this way, but they had never raised her to hate someone based on some preconceived notion either, and that was what her father was expecting her to do when it came to Tristen and his father. She refused to do it.

Maddie pushed those thoughts aside. She only had a small window of time to spend with Tristen, and she did not want to waste any precious moment. Maddie quickly texted Tristen, sharing plans and agreeing on a regular park bench spot as a secret meeting place each evening over the weekend, allowing them just enough time alone without parental eyes watching.

It didn't take Tristan long to show up, and when he did, they both smiled widely under the moonlight. It was so great to be reunited after weeks apart, despite the concerns between them both. As soon as Tristan got close enough to her, she understood why they were drawn to each other — it was like a magnetic pull, two pieces that were opposite yet completed the other.

"Hey, beautiful," he said, sliding next to her on the bench.

Maddie nestled into his side, comforted by his solid presence. "I've missed you."

Tristen pressed a kiss to her temple. "Me too. But we're together now."

They sat in silence for a moment, the weight of their predicament hanging over them. Tristen took her hand, his thumb grazing over her knuckles.

"I wish it could always be like this," Maddie said wistfully.

Tristen nodded. "No disapproving parents. Just you and me."

Maddie thought of her father, his face lined with grief

since losing Makenna. If he knew about Tristen, it would break his heart. Maddie hated that she was doing this to him, but she couldn't seem to help herself. She wished she could get her father to understand, but he seemed so set in his ways.

Tristen seemed to read her thoughts. "We'll figure this out, Maddie. I promise."

She gazed up at the star-filled night sky, but instead of feeling a sense of joy, she felt overwhelmed by sadness and worry. Tristen was sitting beside her, yet it felt like no matter what they did, nothing could break the darkness that had settled over them. They were facing uncertain times, and the stars twinkled like mocking reminders of what they both wanted but could not have.

Maddie turned to Tristen, her eyes glistening. "Do you really think we can make this work? With our parents against us?"

Tristen squeezed her hand reassuringly. "It won't be easy. But I know one thing — I'm not giving up on us."

He gazed at her tenderly, brushing a strand of hair from her face. Maddie's heart swelled, the sincerity in his voice easing her doubts.

"We can just continue to keep it a secret," she said after a moment. "At least until we figure things out."

Tristen considered this, his brow furrowing. "Maybe that's best for now. Avoid a blowup."

Maddie nodded. As much as she hated deception, she couldn't bear to break her father's heart, not after losing Makenna. They had done everything they could to save her, and nothing had been enough, not even the very marrow that ran through Maddie's veins.

"We'll have to be really careful," Tristen said. "No slipping up."

"I know." Maddie leaned against him, drawing strength from his solid frame. "But it'll be worth it. To be together."

Tristen tilted her chin up, meeting her lips in a tender kiss. Maddie melted into him, the world fading away.

When they finally pulled apart, Tristen rested his forehead against hers. "No matter what happens, I'll always be here. I love you, Maddie."

"I love you too," she whispered. And she knew then that their love could conquer any obstacle in their path.

The two of them moved past the bench and headed to the fields where they spent many a summer night. The night air was still, filled only with the soft chirping of crickets. Maddie and Tristen lay side by side in the cool grass, gazing up at the endless expanse of stars above them. The moon was a thin crescent, providing just enough light to make out each other's features.

Maddie inhaled deeply, taking in the earthy scent of soil and grass. A light breeze ruffled her hair, raising goosebumps on her bare arms. She shivered slightly.

Noticing this, Tristen wrapped an arm around her, pulling her close. She nestled against him, comforted by his warmth.

"It's beautiful out here," Tristen murmured.

Maddie nodded, eyes tracing the glittering clusters of stars. "I could stay like this forever."

Tristen squeezed her gently. "Me too."

They lay in the grass, Tristen's arm wrapped protectively around Maddie, her head resting against his chest. The night sky stretched out before them, an endless blanket of stars twinkling in the darkness like tiny pinpricks of light. The crescent moon hung in the sky, casting an ethereal glow on their faces. The stillness was punctuated by occasional rustles of grass or a distant animal cry, but everything faded into insignificance as they took solace in each other's presence.

They were quiet for a time, simply existing together

under the vast night sky. The air was still, save for the gentle rustling of leaves in the breeze and the occasional trill of a night bird. The distant laughter of a child carried on the wind, punctuating the silence. Maddie was aware of Tristen's steady breathing and her own heartbeats echoing in her chest.

Eventually Tristen rolled onto his side, facing Maddie. His eyes searched hers, filled with tenderness. Slowly, he leaned in, lips meeting hers in a soft kiss.

Maddie's pulse quickened, heat rising in her cheeks despite the cool air. She kissed him back firmly, losing herself in the moment.

When they finally broke apart, Tristen stroked her face gently. "I love you, Maddie. No matter what happens, don't forget that."

She placed her hand over his. "I won't. I promise."

Maddie nestled closer against Tristen's chest, listening to the steady thump of his heartbeat. She felt safe here in his arms, like nothing could touch them. After a few moments of contented silence, Maddie spoke softly. "Tristen, do you ever think about running away together?"

He tensed slightly at her words. "Sometimes," he admitted. "But where would we go?"

"Anywhere," Maddie said wistfully. "We could just get in your truck and drive until we find a place that feels right."

Tristen considered this. "It's tempting. But our parents would be worried sick."

Maddie sighed. "I know. I just wish it could be simpler."

"Me too," Tristen murmured, kissing the top of her head.

They lapsed into thoughtful silence again. Then Maddie perked up. "Did I ever tell you about Bonnie and Clyde?"

Tristen looked puzzled. "The outlaws from the 1930s?"

"Yeah," Maddie said. "They were these young lovers

who robbed banks all across the country. My grandma used to tell me stories about them."

"Weren't they shot by the police eventually?" Tristen asked doubtfully.

"Well, yes," Maddie admitted. "But before that, they were free. Riding around with each other against the whole world."

She propped herself up on one elbow, looking earnestly at Tristen. "Don't you think that's kind of romantic, in a way? They only had each other, but it was enough."

Tristen considered this, then nodded slowly. "Yeah, I can see the appeal. Just the two of us on the open road." He smiled. "We'd make a pretty good Bonnie and Clyde."

Maddie's eyes shone. "You think so?"

"I know so." Tristen leaned in and kissed her tenderly.

They held each other close beneath the stars, taking comfort in their love. For now, just being together was enough.

Maddie snuggled against Tristen's chest, listening to the steady beat of his heart. She thought about the story of Bonnie and Clyde, how they'd been willing to sacrifice everything just to be together.

"Do you think we could do it?" she wondered aloud. "Just take off, leave all this behind?"

Tristen was quiet for a moment. "Maybe," he said finally. "If we had to. But only as a last resort."

Maddie nodded, knowing he was right. It was a reckless fantasy, running away. Still, the idea held the allure of forbidden love, a tragic heroine in a novel that would be passed down from generation to generation.

"Bonnie and Clyde had each other," she mused. "Against the whole world, it was those two side-by-side."

She tilted her head back to look Tristen in the eyes. "That's how I feel about us. Like it's you and me against the odds."

Tristen brushed a strand of hair from her face tenderly. "Me too," he said. "We're in this together."

They kissed again, a long, deep kiss under the stars. No matter what came next, they had this moment together. For now, that was enough. Maddie pulled back from the kiss, a worried look in her eyes.

"Do you really think we can make this work?" she asked Tristen. "With my dad so against it, and your parents..."

She trailed off, not wanting to dampen the mood but unable to quell her doubts. Maddie was in her head now, and she couldn't seem to claw her way out of the doubts that were circling inside her.

Tristen squeezed her hand reassuringly. "It won't be easy," he admitted. "But love finds a way, right? We just have to be smart about it."

He gazed at Maddie earnestly. "All I know is I want to be with you. I'm willing to fight for that, no matter what it takes. Are you?"

Maddie was quiet for a moment, considering. Then she met Tristen's eyes with determination.

"Yes," she said firmly. "I'm with you. Whatever comes next, we'll face it together."

Tristen's face lit up with relief and joy. He pulled Maddie close, and she rested her head on his chest once more, comforted by the steady rhythm within. They sat like that for a long time, two young lovers beneath the stars. The future was uncertain, but they had each other. For now, that was enough.

Chapter 23

Maddie stepped into Grandma Minnie's faded yellow living room, her shoulders hunched and hands shoved deep in her jeans pockets. The familiar scent of lavender and old books immediately enveloped her but did little to soothe the knots twisting in her stomach.

She perched on the edge of the floral couch, fingers worrying the hem of her shirt. "Grandma, I...I'm worried that I'll never get to be with Tristen. Ever since Makenna died, Dad just won't let up. It's like he has to double down on his convictions. Why can't he just get over it?"

Maddie glanced up, meeting her grandmother's warm brown eyes. In them, she saw echoes of her own grief yet also strength. "I'm scared I'm going to lose him. That he'll get tired of dealing with all my baggage."

Her voice broke on the last word. Grandma Minnie reached over and squeezed her hand, the paper-thin skin comforting in its familiarity.

"Oh, sweetie, relationships aren't easy, especially at your age. But the real deal, the forever kind of love? It can weather any storm. You just have to trust in it."

Maddie managed a small smile, reassured by her grandmother's quiet wisdom. For a moment, the knots loosened. She wasn't alone in this — she had Grandma Minnie, just as she'd always had. They would get through this, just like they got through everything else. Together. Part of her worried that her father would never forgive Grandma Minnie if he found out that she had aided and abetted Maddie with her relationship with Tristen. It was wrong of her to do all the things she was doing. Makenna probably would never have gone against her father's wishes. That was something he would certainly throw in her face when he finally figured it out. Maddie would deserve everything he threw at her, because, deep down, she knew she was a disappointment in so many ways.

Grandma Minnie leaned back against the couch cushions with a soft sigh. "You know, your grandpa and I had our fair share of troubles, too, when we were young. He was a soldier, shipped off to Vietnam when we were barely more than kids ourselves."

She gazed out the window, lost in memories. "I was so scared I'd lose him over there. The not knowing was the worst of it — weeks with no letters, no calls. And when he did write, he couldn't tell me much that wasn't blacked out by the censors."

Maddie watched her grandmother's face crease with remembered pain and reached over to squeeze her hand in return.

"But we got through it," Grandma Minnie continued, her voice growing warm. "Every time he came home on leave, it was like falling in love all over again. And the letters I did get, I must've read a hundred times over. All those little ways we had of showing we still cared, even from a world away."

She turned back to Maddie, eyes glistening. "What I'm trying to say is real love finds a way. You and Tristen will figure it out, too. Just don't give up on each other."

Maddie felt a lump rising in her throat. She nodded, unable to speak, then wrapped her arms around her grandmother in a fierce hug. For now, it was enough to simply feel supported. The rest would come in time.

Maddie held on for a long moment, drawing strength from her grandmother's embrace. When she finally pulled back, she wiped at her eyes. "Thanks, Grandma. I really needed to hear that today."

Grandma Minnie patted her hand. "I know, sweetheart. That's what I'm here for."

Maddie managed a small smile. Talking it through had lifted some of the weight from her shoulders. She felt like she could breathe a little easier now. The guilt that weighed her down was a little lighter, too.

"I won't try to force things with Tristen," she said. "But I'll keep holding on to hope. And I'll remember what you said — real love finds a way."

Grandma Minnie's eyes crinkled at the corners. "Thatta girl. One step at a time."

Maddie nodded. With her grandmother's steadying presence, the future seemed less daunting. The ache of missing her sister was still there, but it no longer threatened to swallow her whole. She knew the grief would come in waves. But today, she had found a moment of peace.

Maddie took a deep breath and met her grandmother's kind eyes. "Grandma, how did you know that Grandpa was the one for you? Even when you had to be apart during the war?"

Grandma Minnie smiled wistfully. "Oh, I just knew, deep down. From our very first date, there was a connection between us that I'd never felt with anyone else."

She gazed out the window, lost in memory. "We only had that one evening together before he shipped out. But we talked for hours about our families, our dreams, everything under the sun. I felt like I could tell him anything."

Maddie leaned forward, captivated by the faraway look in her grandmother's eyes. Maddie understood that feeling. She felt the same way with Tristen. He understood her in ways that no one else ever had. Tristen didn't run from her grief when she came to Mellow Creek. He had embraced it and been there for all of it.

"And then he had to go off and fight, and all we had were letters. But every day, I'd wait by the mailbox, hoping for word from him. And whenever I got a letter, it was like hearing his voice again."

Grandma Minnie blinked, coming back to the present. "I missed him so terribly. But even with miles between us, I knew — he was it for me. My heart knew before my head did."

She patted Maddie's hand again. "When it's real, you just know. It's like coming home."

Maddie felt her throat tighten as she looked into her grandmother's wise and knowing eyes. She could feel the intensity of her grandmother's words, like a warm embrace, even as tears began to form in her eyes.

"I think..." she began tentatively. "I think that's how it feels with Tristen. Like I can tell him anything. Like home."

Grandma Minnie nodded. "Then trust that, sweetheart. If your heart knows it's right, have faith. True love always finds its way."

Maddie hugged her grandmother again, feeling a spark of hope flickering back to life inside her. Grandma Minnie's story had given her the answer she needed — have patience, have courage, and above all, have faith.

"Thank you, Grandma," Maddie said, her voice thick with emotion. "For everything. For listening and for sharing your story. I know it wasn't easy."

Grandma Minnie squeezed her hand. "Of course, sweet pea. That's what grandmas are for."

Maddie let out a shaky breath, feeling some of the weight lift off her shoulders. She had been so worried about drifting apart from Tristen, so scared that the distance and time apart would change things between them. But hearing about Grandma Minnie's unshakeable faith in her soldier helped put things in perspective. Maddie's problems were just normal teenage worries, not the end of the world. She was determined to not give up on him, trusting that with patience, the two of them could push through this drought of turmoil they had found themselves in.

"I'm glad I came over today," Maddie said. "I feel better getting all this off my chest. It's nice to know I'm not the only one who's gone through this."

Grandma Minnie chuckled. "Oh, we've all been there. Your old grandma included."

She gave Maddie a playful wink. "Chin up, buttercup. You've got your whole life ahead of you. This is just one chapter."

Maddie smiled, feeling truly relieved for the first time in weeks. Grandma Minnie was right — she and Tristen had so many more chapters left to write.

Maddie stepped forward and wrapped her arms around Grandma Minnie, hugging her tightly. Minnie returned the embrace, patting Maddie's back in that comforting way only grandmas can. Maddie closed her eyes, breathing in the familiar scent of Minnie's perfume — a light, floral fragrance that always reminded her of sunny spring days. It made her think of better times, before Makenna got sick when their family was whole and carefree.

She felt Minnie's bony shoulder blades through the crocheted shawl draped around her petite frame. Maddie was struck by how small and fragile her grandmother felt, like a little bird in her arms. But Grandma Minnie had a strength in her spirit that defied her age and diminishing health. She was a fighter, just like Makenna had been. Maddie swallowed against the lump in her throat as she thought of her twin. God, she missed her. Makenna would've loved talking through all this drama with Tristen. She was always the logical, rational one.

"Thank you," Maddie whispered, her voice muffled against Minnie's shoulder.

Minnie rubbed her back. "You're going to be okay, sweetheart. It might not seem like it now, but you have so much life ahead of you."

Maddie clung to her grandmother, drawing courage from her words. She could do this — she could be strong like Makenna. She just needed to take it one day at a time.

As Maddie pulled away, she caught a glimpse of herself in the mirror that hung on the opposite wall. She looked tired, with dark circles under her eyes and tangled hair. But she also looked determined, like she had a newfound sense of purpose.

Taking a deep breath, Maddie turned to face her grandmother once more. "You're right, Grandma. I have so much life ahead of me. And I'm not going to waste any more of it worrying about things I can't control. I know what I want and who I want to be with."

Grandma Minnie beamed at her. "That's the spirit! You deserve to be happy, Maddie. Don't ever let anyone tell you different."

Maddie nodded, feeling a flicker of hope grow into a flame inside her chest. "I won't, Grandma. I promise."

She hugged her grandmother once more before heading towards the door. "Thank you again for everything. I love you."

"I love you too, sweet pea," Grandma Minnie called after her as she stepped onto the porch.

Maddie took a deep breath of crisp autumn air, feeling renewed and ready to face whatever came her way. She knew there would still be challenges, still be moments of grief and doubt. But with Grandma Minnie's love and guidance, Maddie felt like she could handle anything life threw at her.

Chapter 24

The sun streamed through the sheer curtains, casting a warm glow over Maddie's bedroom. The cheerful chirping of birds outside her window only served to sharpen the contrast between the sunny day and the storm raging inside her. Maddie sat on the edge of her bed, sobbing into her hands, her shoulders shaking with the weight of her grief. Her twin sister, Makenna, had been gone for only eight months now, but the pain felt as fresh as it did on the day she passed. Next week would be her eighteenth birthday, and she had never had one without her sister.

But that wasn't the only thing that made her feel so out of sorts. It was so much more than that. Running around and lying to her parents was eating away at her conscience. If that wasn't bad enough, the idea that Grandma Minnie was covering for her made her stomach churn. If her father found out, he would never forgive his mother. If the two of them lost their relationship over this, Maddie would never forgive herself. All these lives could be ruined because she refused to give up Tristen. Maddie felt selfish, lost, and alone.

"Sweetheart, are you okay? Can I come in?" Robert Tyler, Maddie's father, knocked softly on her door, concern lacing his voice.

"Leave me alone," Maddie choked out between sobs, barely able to catch her breath. She couldn't bear to face her father right now, not when her heart felt like it was being torn apart at the seams. All her emotions raced through her like a cyclone. Maddie didn't feel safe around him right now. She would be too tempted to confess her sins, and her world could come crashing down all over again.

"We're here for you, Maddie," he spoke through the door. Maddie heard him sigh before he stepped away from the door.

Maddie's chest tightened as she gasped for air, her lungs seemingly unable to get enough oxygen. It felt like everything was suffocating her — the loss of her sister, the disapproval from her parents about her secret relationship with Tristen, and the pressure of keeping her relationship hidden. Everything was closing in on her, and there was nothing to do but let it swallow her whole.

"Why did you have to go?" she whispered hoarsely, her voice breaking under the strain of her tears. "I need you, Makenna."

Maddie's thoughts swirled around her like a hurricane, threatening to pull her under. She pictured Tristen's face, his warm smile, and the way he held her close during their stolen moments together. But even those memories were tainted by the secret they shared — a secret Maddie knew her parents would never approve of.

She buried her face in her pillow, letting her tears soak into the fabric. She longed for the days when everything was simpler, when she and Makenna were free to laugh and enjoy life without the shadow of cancer hanging over them.

"Maybe it's better if we just end things now," Maddie whispered to herself through her sobs. The thought of losing Tristen, too, was unbearable, but she couldn't help but wonder if keeping their relationship a secret was only adding to her pain.

As the sun continued to shine brightly outside, the

world seemingly oblivious to her anguish, Maddie let the tears flow, feeling as though she was sinking deeper and deeper into the darkness that threatened to swallow her whole. The incessant ticking of the clock echoed in Maddie's ears as she lay on her bed, staring at the ceiling. The sun poured through her window, casting warm, golden rays across her tear-streaked face. She took shallow breaths, her chest tightening with each one. It felt as if the weight of the world was pressing down on her, threatening to crush her.

When her phone rang, Maddie almost didn't answer it. She cleared her throat and picked up the call. "Hello?"

"Hey, Maddie," Tristen's voice came through her phone speaker, his usual warmth subdued. "How are you holding up?"

Maddie hesitated, her fingers gripping the edges of her blanket. "I don't know, Tristen. I feel like I'm drowning, and there's no way out."

"Talk to me," he urged gently, the concern evident in his voice.

"Everything is just…too much," Maddie whispered, her words catching in her throat. "My parents, my sister, and now us. I can't help but wonder if we're making a mistake."

"Are you saying you want to end things?" Tristen asked cautiously, his voice barely above a whisper.

Maddie bit her lip, her heart aching at the thought. "I don't want to lose you, Tristen. But I'm scared that if we keep going like this, it'll only make things worse."

"Maybe we can find a way to be together without hiding," Tristen suggested, desperation seeping into his tone. "We can figure it out, I promise."

"Can we, though?" Maddie questioned, her voice hollow. "I don't know if there's any way for us to be together without causing more pain."

Tristen was silent for a moment, and Maddie could

almost hear him wrestling with his own thoughts. "I don't know," he finally admitted. "But I'm willing to try if you are."

"Maybe..." Maddie hesitated, her heart aching with indecision. "Maybe we just need some time to think."

"Okay," Tristen agreed quietly, his voice filled with unspoken emotion. "Just know that I love you, Maddie. And I'll be here when you're ready."

"Thank you," she whispered, her eyes filling with fresh tears. "I love you too."

As they hung up, Maddie's gaze drifted back to the ceiling, the sunlight filtering through her window casting gently swaying patterns on it. She couldn't shake the feeling that despite their words of reassurance, a dark cloud loomed over their future, threatening to tear them apart.

Maddie stood in front of the bathroom mirror, her tear-filled eyes staring back at her. Her hands trembled as she gripped the edge of the counter, the weight of her emotions threatening to pull her under. The steady drip of the faucet filled the room, echoing her unshed tears.

"Maybe it's better if we just end things now," Maddie whispered to her reflection, a sob catching in her throat. Her parents' disapproval hung over her like a dark cloud, casting an ever-growing shadow on her relationship with Tristen. She couldn't bear the thought of losing him, but the isolation and despair that came with hiding their love was becoming too much to bear.

Her father's voice rang through her memory. "You need to focus on your future, Maddie. Not on some boy who has no place in it."

"Where is he now?" her mother had asked, the judgment clear in her eyes. "Where is this 'perfect boy' when you're crying yourself to sleep?"

Maddie squeezed her eyes shut, trying to block out the harsh words. But they only served to amplify her fears, solidifying the doubts that had begun to creep in. How could she and Tristen have a future together when the world seemed so determined to keep them apart?

"I don't know how much longer I can do this," Maddie murmured, her fingers tracing the cool porcelain of the sink.

Maddie plopped down on her bed and curled up in a ball. She wasn't sure how long it took her to finally fall asleep. For once, her night was dreamless. That was something she was thankful for, at least.

The morning sun streamed through the curtains, casting a warm golden glow across Maddie's bedroom. Birds sang their cheerful melodies outside her window, but their songs did nothing to ease the turmoil that churned within her. Her thoughts were a tangled mess, weighed down by her parents' disapproval and the strain of her secret relationship.

"Ugh," she muttered, dragging herself out of bed and pulling her favorite hoodie over her head. The soft fabric felt like a protective shield against the world. Maddie glanced at the clock, realizing that if she didn't leave soon, she'd be late for church again.

"Maybe I just won't go today," she whispered to herself, her voice barely audible even in the silence of her room. As the thought took root, she felt a strange sense of relief wash over her. One day, not to be surrounded by a crowd of people and pretend that everything was all right.

Maddie walked downstairs and saw her mom at the table. "You ready, Maddie?"

"I want to stay home today if that's ok," Maddie asked her mom. She hardly ever stayed home from church, only on the rare occasion.

Her mom took one look at her and saw the way she was dressed. "You look like you need a day."

"Thanks, Mom." Maddie wrapped her arms around her and gave her a hug.

"Hey, you know you can talk to me, right?" Her mom added.

"Yeah," Maddie answered half-heartedly. Her mom might have thought she could, but Maddie didn't feel like she could trust herself to talk to anyone right now. "I'm just going to spend some time in town, okay?"

"Sure, baby. Take some time."

When her parents left, Maddie started off on her own. As she wandered aimlessly through the town, Maddie couldn't help but feel a pang of guilt for everything that had happened since she had come to Mellow Creek. If it wasn't bad enough that her sister's illness had torn her family apart, she was testing what was left of their relationship. What was wrong with her?

"Can we really keep this up?" she wondered, her thoughts drifting back to their conversation the night before. Her heart ached with longing for the simplicity of earlier days when she could laugh with Tristen without fear or guilt, tainting their happiness. But those days were gone, replaced by an endless labyrinth of secrets and lies. Maddie's once-sturdy support system had crumbled, leaving her feeling isolated and adrift. She knew she couldn't go on like this forever, but she also didn't know how to find her way out of the darkness.

"Where do we go from here?" Maddie whispered to herself, sinking down onto a park bench. As she watched children laughing and playing in the sunlight, she clung to the hope that she and Tristen would somehow find a path through the storm.

The afternoon sun filtered through the trees at the park, casting dappled shadows on the ground as Maddie sat on a bench, her fingers gently tracing the wood grain. She watched children playing and running freely, their laughter filling the air. Her heart swelled with nostalgia as she remembered a time when life was simpler before everything had fallen apart.

She remembered the time when Tristen had joined her and Makenna one winter day when they were staying with Grandma Minnie. They had been only eight, bundled up against the cold, spending hours creating a lopsided snowman that had ultimately collapsed under its own weight. It had been one of those days that had felt like magic—perfect and carefree.

"Those were the good times," she whispered, her eyes welling up with tears.

"Talking to yourself now?" Tristen's voice cut through her reverie, snapping her back to reality. He stood before her, hands tucked into his pockets, concern etched on his face.

"Tristen, I…" she began hesitantly, but he cut her off.

"Look, I know things have been rough lately," he admitted, rubbing the back of his neck. "But we'll get through this together, okay?"

"Will we?" Maddie challenged, her emotions bubbling to the surface. "It feels like every time we try to talk, we just end up arguing!"

"Maybe if you'd actually open up to me instead of shutting me out all the time, things would be different," Tristen shot back, frustration evident in his tone.

"Open up to you?" Maddie scoffed. "My sister is gone, my parents disapprove of our relationship, and I'm drowning in my own pain! How much more do you want from me, Tristen?"

"Hey, hey," Tristen said, holding his hands up in surrender. "I'm not the enemy here, Maddie. I just want to help."

Maddie sighed. "I know."

"Listen," Tristen began hesitantly, "I know we haven't been communicating well lately. But I want you to know that I'm here for you, okay?"

"Are you?" Maddie whispered, her eyes brimming with tears. "Because it feels like I'm losing you too, Tristen."

"Hey, don't say that," Tristen replied, wrapping an arm around her shoulders. "I love you, Maddie."

She looked up into his eyes, searching for reassurance. "Do you think we can make it through this? Together?"

Tristen sighed, running a hand through his hair. "I don't know, Maddie. I really don't. But I'm willing to try if you are."

A tear slipped down her cheek as she stared out at the world beyond her window, so tantalizingly close yet impossibly distant. "I'm just so tired, Tristen," she admitted, her voice barely audible. "Tired of fighting, tired of hurting, tired of feeling like everything is falling apart."

"I know," he murmured, pulling her closer. "But we have to keep going, Maddie. For each other."

"You're right."

"Let's just focus on getting through today, okay?"

"Okay," Maddie agreed, but the uncertainty still lingered in her eyes as they held onto each other, desperately seeking solace in a world that seemed determined to tear them apart. And as they stood there, wrapped in each other's arms, the future remained uncertain.

Chapter 25

Tristen stood beneath the shadow of the old maple tree, the rustle of its leaves whispering secrets he wished he could understand. He clenched his fists, his nails digging into his palms as he tried to make sense of the tangled web of emotions that threatened to suffocate him.

He couldn't shake the feeling that his love for Maddie was a betrayal, not just to his family but to her own. Their families had grown up in the same small town, each one with its own set of bitter resentments and long-held grudges. Tristen's father had never forgiven Robert Tyler for him being benched during the championship game in his senior year of high school. That was a defining game, one that would have locked in his scholarship to college. Instead, his father had become a car salesman, chasing a different dream altogether. Maddie's father still held on to a simmering anger over the same football drama, something that should have been left on the field years ago. The tension between the two families was palpable, a constant undercurrent threatening to pull Tristen and Maddie apart at any moment.

Tristen's heart ached when he thought of the pain Maddie had already endured after losing her twin sister, Makenna, to leukemia. The memory of her grief-stricken face haunted him, making him question whether his love was worth the potential heartbreak it could cause both their families. Today, they were meeting at the library, their secret cover no one had bothered to question before.

"Hey, Tristen," Maddie said softly, appearing beside him. Her eyes searched his face, worry creasing her brow. "What's going on? You seem...distant."

"Nothing," he lied, forcing a smile. "Just lost in thought."

Maddie reached out, taking his hand in hers. "You know you can talk to me about anything," she said, her voice gentle and unwavering. "I'm here for you."

Tristen looked down at their intertwined fingers, marveling at how perfectly they fit together. He wanted to pour out his fears and doubts, to let Maddie soothe them away with her quiet strength. But he couldn't bring himself to burden her with his troubles, not when she had already suffered so much.

"Thanks, Maddie," he murmured, giving her hand a reassuring squeeze. "I appreciate that."

Maddie offered him a small smile, but the worry lingered in her eyes. Tristen knew she could sense his turmoil, and it pained him to keep the truth from her. "Let's get out of here."

"Okay, but we have to stay out of sight," agreed Maddie.

As they walked together, the weight of their families' animosity bore down on Tristen like an oppressive storm cloud. He desperately wanted to break free, to prove to everyone that love could conquer all — even a decades-long feud. But the fear of causing more pain gnawed at him, threatening to tear his resolve apart.

"Promise me something," Maddie said suddenly, stopping beneath the maple tree. She looked up at him, her brown eyes filled with determination. "Promise me that no matter what happens, we'll always fight for each other."

Tristen stared into her eyes, seeing the fierce love and unwavering commitment that shone in them. In that moment, he felt a flicker of hope ignite within him — a burning flame that refused to be extinguished by doubt and despair.

"I promise," he whispered, pulling her close. As they embraced beneath the whispering leaves, Tristen vowed to himself that he would do everything in his power to protect and cherish the love they shared. No matter the cost.

After leaving Maddie, he returned home, where he contemplated his options. The sky was a muted gray, casting a somber mood over the neighborhood as Tristen stood on his front porch, the wooden steps creaking beneath him. With each passing day, the rift between his family and the Tylers seemed to grow wider, threatening to swallow any hope of reconciliation. As he stared at the bleak landscape, the cold November wind nipped at his cheeks and tugged at his resolve.

"Those Tylers," he heard his father's voice boom from inside the house, followed by the distinct sound of his fist slamming against the kitchen table. "They'll never be anything but trouble."

Tristen's heart clenched, the bitter words stinging like shards of glass. He knew his father had always held a deep-seated resentment for the Tyler family, but hearing it so blatantly made him doubt the strength of his relationship with Maddie even more.

"They're just using that girl's tragedy to get sympathy from everyone, I bet," his father continued, his voice laced with disdain. "Well, they won't fool me."

"Is that really what you think?" Tristen asked himself, his thoughts plagued by conflicting emotions as he considered Maddie's grief over her sister's loss. A gust of wind tore through the air, mirroring the turmoil in his heart.

As much as he wanted to prove his father wrong, Tristen

knew he couldn't simply confront him. The stubbornness that ran through their family was a formidable barrier, one that would require careful dismantling. And so, a plan began to form in his mind: a plan to change his father's perspective on the Tylers and show him that love could heal even the deepest wounds.

"Hey, Dad," Tristen called as he re-entered the house, his voice steady despite the storm raging within him. "Do you think you could help me with something?"

"Sure, what do you need?" his father replied, the gruffness in his tone momentarily softened by curiosity.

"I want to show support to Maddie Tyler. Their family is hosting a fundraiser for leukemia research in a few weeks," Tristen said, watching his father's face carefully for any signs of resistance. "I think it would be a good opportunity to learn more about the disease that took Makenna."

His father frowned, clearly torn between his contempt for the Tylers and his innate sense of duty as a parent. But before he could voice an objection, Tristen continued, "It's not about them, Dad. It's about understanding what Maddie went through and showing our support. No one should have to lose a loved one to leukemia."

"It's the right thing to do, Daniel. Most of the town will be showing up," added his mom.

"Alright," his father finally conceded, his expression still clouded with reluctance. "We'll go. But that doesn't mean I'm donating anything."

"Thank you," Tristen replied, his heart swelling with a newfound determination. He knew the road ahead would be fraught with obstacles, but for Maddie and the love they shared, he was willing to take the risk. Just getting the two men in the same room was half the battle.

As the wind howled outside, Tristen felt the embers of hope begin to burn brighter within him. With every step he took towards bridging the gap between their families, he believed, more than ever, that love could conquer all. And as he stood in the dimly lit hallway, the shadows cast by the gray sky seemed just a little less oppressive.

The sun dipped below the horizon, casting long shadows across Tristen's bedroom floor. He lay on his bed, fingers entwined behind his head, staring up at the ceiling. The room was filled with the fading light of day, painting everything in a soft golden glow. But the beauty of the moment was lost on him, his mind consumed by the turmoil of emotions swirling within.

"Is it really worth it?" he whispered to himself, the words barely audible. "Can I fight for something that might only cause more pain?"

His thoughts wandered to Maddie, her eyes shimmering with unshed tears as she spoke about Makenna. He knew the weight of her loss still hung heavily upon her shoulders. Was his love enough to ease that burden? Or would their relationship only serve to widen the rift between their families, causing more heartache?

Tristen sat up and swung his legs over the side of the bed, burying his face in his hands. He needed to weigh the potential consequences of his actions to consider the risks and benefits before making a decision that could alter the course of not just his life but Maddie's as well.

"Okay," he muttered, taking a deep breath and attempting to clear his mind. "What are the risks?"

The most obvious risk was his father's disapproval. Tristen knew that going against his father's wishes would strain their relationship, possibly beyond repair. Would his father ever accept the Tylers, or would their feud continue to fester? And what about Maddie's father? If he couldn't change Mr. Tyler's opinion of his family either, their relationship would be doomed from the start.

"Benefits," he murmured, trying to shift his focus. Being with Maddie brought happiness and a sense of completeness to his life that Tristen hadn't known was missing until they found each other. Her strength in the face of adversity was an inspiration, a living testament to the power of love and resilience. Together, they could face anything life threw at them.

Later, Tristen stood in the dimly lit hallway outside his bedroom, his chest tightening as he grappled with a whirlwind of emotions. The wallpaper, adorned with an intricate pattern of faded flowers, seemed to close in on him, making it difficult to breathe. He leaned against the wall, pressing his forehead against the cool surface as he tried to calm his racing heart. He could hear his parents talking in the living room.

"That Tyler girl is nothing but trouble. She'll bring nothing but pain to this family," came his father's voice from the living room, anger lacing each syllable.

His father's words echoed in Tristen's mind, fueling his internal conflict. He had been struggling with the decision to pursue his relationship with Maddie, knowing that it could potentially cause strife between their families. Now, hearing his father's harsh judgment, the weight of his decision grew heavier.

Frustration and sadness swirled within Tristen as he clenched his fists, feeling the pressure of his family's expectations bearing down on him. They wanted him to stay away from the Tyler family to avoid the heartache they believed would inevitably follow. But how could he turn his back on Maddie, the girl who had captured his heart and shown him the true meaning of love?

"Daniel," his mother's voice chimed in, softer than his father's but still firm in her conviction. "We were young once. Don't you remember what it felt like? And why are you blaming that poor child for anything that happened when you were in high school. She wasn't even born."

"He's taking too many risks with his future. Did you know he wants to minor in art now? He's become so distracted since that girl came into his life. She's brought the worst out in him."

"He's wrong," he whispered to himself, the words barely audible even to his own ears. "Maddie brings out the best."

Tristen wanted to confront his father, but he knew it wouldn't do any good. His words only confirmed that it was best that he keep his relationship a secret. Tristen didn't want his father to ruin this, just like he ruined every other dream in his life. He couldn't help but feel the pain of rejection in his dad's words. His father had never believed in his art. It was clear to him now that he never would, and that knowledge cut him like a knife. If only there was a way to get out of here and leave his past behind. Tristen would give anything to start fresh somewhere else where his father couldn't taint him with his toxicity. Someday, he would have that world, a beautiful one where he and Maddie could support each other and live the life they were supposed to be living.

Later, Tristen lay sprawled on his bed, staring at the ceiling fan as it spun lazily above him. The sun cast a warm glow through the curtains, bathing the room in a hazy gold. He looked at a picture on his phone, taken this summer when they had spent hours laughing as they splashed each other at the pond, their smiles wide and genuine. He couldn't help but trace over her features, noting how her eyes sparkled with life, contrasting with the sadness that now lingered as memories of Makenna were raw in her mind since her birthday.

A pang of emotion stirred deep within Tristen's chest, making it difficult to breathe. He realized that he couldn't imagine a world without Maddie in it. Her laughter, her strength, her ability to find beauty in the smallest things —

all of these qualities made her an irreplaceable presence in his life. He wanted nothing more than to bring back the joy she once embodied, to see her smile again as she did in that photograph.

An idea began to form in his mind, one that could potentially rekindle the light in Maddie's eyes. It was risky, but he was willing to take that chance if it meant seeing her happy. Tristen decided that he would plan a grand romantic gesture, a secret rendezvous for the two of them to search for the hidden treasure that local legends spoke about. He knew Maddie loved mystery and adventure, and perhaps this would be the perfect distraction from the pain she was experiencing.

That was when he started printing out every version of any map he could find. There were many blogs about the caverns and the bank robbers who had left their loot behind somewhere in the cavern's depths. No one had ever found it, but that didn't mean it wasn't there. Miracles could happen. It started with a little bit of hope and a whole lot of conviction.

As Tristen began to plan their secret rendezvous, he couldn't help but envision Maddie by his side, her face alight with excitement and curiosity. Together, they would embark on an unforgettable journey, searching for a hidden treasure that remained shrouded in mystery. And perhaps, along the way, they would rediscover the love that had always existed between them, a love that defied even the darkest of times. Right now, they needed that light between them if their relationship was going to survive.

Tristen stood nervously in front of the library, waiting for Maddie to arrive. She was taking longer than usual, and Tristen was trying to not take that as a bad sign.

"Hey, Tristen," Maddie greeted him with a small smile, trying to hide the shadows beneath her eyes.

"Hi, Maddie. I have something special planned for us,"

Tristen said, meeting her gaze. "I thought we could go on an adventure together, just the two of us."

Maddie's eyes widened with curiosity. "What kind of adventure?"

"Something that'll take your mind off things, even if it's just for a little while," he explained, unfolding the map and revealing the hidden treasure marked on it. "This is one of the maps I found of the cavern. This is where they think the treasure might be."

"Wow," Maddie breathed, her fingers tracing the lines on the worn parchment. "When do you want to go?"

"Tomorrow morning. We'll meet at the edge of the woods at 6 a.m." His heart pounded in his chest as he awaited Maddie's response.

"Okay, I'm in," she agreed, her voice tinged with excitement. "Works perfect. I'll just tell them I'm spending the day with Lydia."

"Great!" Tristen grinned, feeling the first spark of hope ignite within him. "It'll be something we'll never forget."

Chapter 26

The following morning, the sun had barely risen when Tristen and Maddie met at their designated spot. The two made their way to his truck so they could drive to the nature preserve.

"Are you ready for the adventure of a lifetime?" asked Tristen.

"As soon as I get the rest of this coffee in me." Maddie took another drink and hoped the caffeine would do its trick. She hadn't slept well last night as she thought about what they would be doing all night. Part of her wished Makenna was with her. She and her twin had dreamt about tackling these caves forever. If Makenna were here, there would have been no holding her back on this adventure. Maddie was sure of it.

When they finally made it to the nature preserve, Maddie's brain was starting to fully waken. She took in the world around her, memorizing every inch of their surroundings so she could remember this moment for the rest of her life. The air was cool and fragrant with dew as they began their trek through the woods, guided by the ancient map.

"The entrance should be right up there. We marked it before." Maddie said, slightly out of breath as they navigated the uneven terrain.

As they rounded a bend in the path, Maddie caught

a glimpse of the overgrowth that surrounded the cavern entrance.

"Well, here we are. This time, we're going inside." Maddie felt a jolt of excitement race through her.

"Are you ready for this?" Tristen smiled, taking her hand and leading her closer to the entrance.

"Yes! Thank you for bringing me here, Tristen." Maddie's voice was soft but filled with gratitude. "I can feel my sister's presence here. It's like she's with us on this adventure."

Maddie felt a warmth spread through her. She had a feeling it was going to be the best day ever. Together, they would explore the depths of the caverns and seek out the hidden treasure that awaited them, all the while allowing their love to grow and heal the wounds that life had left behind.

The cavern walls seemed to come alive as sunlight filtered through the entrance, casting intricate shadows on the rough surfaces. Maddie felt a sense of wonder as she took in the sight, her fingers lightly brushing against the cool rocks.

"Maddie," he said, turning to face her, "what's the story behind this hidden treasure anyway?"

Maddie leaned against the rock wall, her eyes gleaming with excitement as he began to share the tale. "Legend has it that centuries ago, two love-stricken bandits robbed several banks."

"Like Bonnie and Clyde?" suggested Tristen.

"Something like that. They hid the majority of their loot inside the cavern walls and were set to return to it but met a tragic end. Not quite like Bonnie and Clyde, though. They actually died in a fire, not being shot to pieces in their getaway car."

"Still tragic," added Tristen.

"Yes. Most definitely," agreed Maddie.

"Their loss just might be our gain." Tristen gazed

around the cavern. "I think it's worth searching for, at least. And even if we don't find the treasure, maybe we'll find something else just as valuable."

Maddie nodded, her heart swelling with love for Tristen and appreciation for the adventure they were embarking on together. "Let's start looking, then."

Together, they ventured deeper into the caverns, following the map's cryptic clues and piecing together the puzzle before them. The air grew cooler as they progressed, and their footsteps echoed off the walls, creating an eerie yet oddly comforting rhythm. At one point, they faced a fork in the path, with two equally dark and foreboding tunnels stretching out before them. Maddie hesitated, her pulse quickening as she considered the choice before them.

"Which way do you think we should go?" she asked Tristen, her voice wavering slightly.

He studied the map carefully, his brow furrowed in concentration. "I think...this way," he declared, pointing to the tunnel on the right.

"Are you sure?" Maddie questioned, her eyes searching his face for any doubt.

"Trust me," he reassured her, offering a comforting smile. "We're in this together."

As they navigated the twists and turns of the caverns, overcoming obstacles that threatened to impede their progress, Maddie found herself reflecting on the journey that had led her here. She thought of Makenna, of the love and laughter they'd shared, and how her sister's spirit seemed to be guiding them through these dark passages. But it was also Tristen who had brought her here, who had given her a reason to hope again amidst the pain. And as they continued their search for the hidden treasure, Maddie couldn't help but feel that perhaps the greatest gift of all was not the treasure they sought but the love they were discovering along the way.

Maddie's heart pounded in her chest as they stood on the precipice of a vast underground chamber, its walls encrusted with glittering minerals that danced under the beam of their flashlight. The air was thick and heavy, imbued with both danger and hope. She turned to Tristen, her eyes wide with awe and trepidation, and took her hand gently in his. "We've got this, right?"

"Before we go any further," he began, "there's something I need to say."

Maddie looked at him expectantly, her fingers tightening around his as she waited for him to continue.

"Ever since Makenna's passing, I've watched you carry so much pain and grief. It's been tearing me apart to see you hurting like this," Tristen confessed, his throat tightening. "I know I can't replace your sister or take away your pain, but I want to be there for you, to help you heal and find happiness again."

Tears welled up in Maddie's eyes, and she squeezed Tristen's hand gratefully. "Thank you. You've already helped me more than you know."

A small smile graced Tristen's lips, a flicker of hope igniting in his heart. "This adventure isn't just about finding treasure. I wanted to prove to you that life still has incredible experiences to offer and that I'll be by your side through it all."

As they shared the intimate moment, Tristen recalled the meticulous preparations he'd made for their rendezvous. He'd spent countless hours poring over maps and gathering supplies, ensuring they had everything they needed for their journey into the unknown. From climbing gear and sturdy hiking boots to flashlights and a first aid kit, he'd taken every precaution to ensure their safety in pursuit of the treasure.

"Are you ready?" Tristen asked softly, his eyes searching Maddie's face for any lingering doubt.

Maddie nodded, her gaze resolute. "Let's do this."

Maddie hesitated at the entrance to the next area, the cave's darkness beckoning her like a long-lost friend. Tristen stood beside her, his hand warm and reassuring in hers, as they prepared to explore the narrow passages together.

"Ready?" he asked, his voice soft and steady.

"Ready," she whispered back, though her heart raced with excitement and fear.

As they ventured deeper into the cave, Maddie's eyes slowly adjusted to the dimness, revealing the jagged edges of the walls that seemed ready to bite them. The air was thick and damp, making it difficult to breathe. Maddie couldn't help but think of her sister, Makenna, who had fought for every breath in her final days. Was this how it had felt to not be able to catch her breath?

"Watch your step," Tristen warned, guiding her around a particularly treacherous section. "These rocks can be slippery."

"Thanks," she murmured, grateful for his presence. She knew this adventure was partly an attempt to distract herself, but it also felt like a rite of passage — a way to prove that she could face her fears head-on. As they moved further into the darkness, the air seemed to hum with a strange tension, the weight of a thousand secrets hidden within the shadows. The echo of their footsteps mingled with the distant drip of water, creating an eerie soundtrack to their journey.

"Remember the first time we came here?" Tristen asked, his voice tinged with nostalgia. "Can you imagine trying to lead the others through here?"

"Yeah," Maddie replied, smiling at the memory. "That would have been a nightmare."

Suddenly, without warning, the ceiling above them groaned, and rocks and debris began to fall. Maddie barely had time to register what was happening before Tristen shoved her out of the way, his shout muffled by the sound of crashing stone.

"Tristen!" she screamed, her voice barely audible over the cacophony.

"Stay back, Maddie!" he shouted, his eyes wide with fear. "I'll find a way around!"

As the dust settled, Maddie realized that they were separated by a wall of fallen rock, trapping her in a small pocket of darkness. Panic surged through her, making it even more difficult to breathe. She clawed at the rocks, her fingers bleeding as she desperately tried to dig her way out, but it was no use — the weight of the debris was too much for her to move.

"Tristen," she whispered, tears streaming down her face. "I'm so scared."

"Stay strong, Maddie," his voice came through faintly, muffled by the barrier between them. "We'll get out of this, I promise."

As she leaned against the cold stone, her breath ragged and her heart heavy, Maddie felt a familiar wave of despair wash over her. She had already lost Makenna, and now she faced the very real possibility of losing Tristen as well. The hopelessness threatened to consume her, but somewhere deep inside, a tiny ember of determination still burned. As Maddie's tears mixed with the dust on her cheeks, a faint glow began to fill the small cavern. She wiped her eyes, thinking it was just her imagination playing tricks on her. But when she looked up, there stood Makenna, her twin sister, as radiant as ever.

"Kenna?" Maddie breathed in disbelief, her heartache momentarily forgotten. Before, she had only imagined her. This time, it was different. A warmth washed over her, calming all her fears.

"Hey, Mads," Makenna smiled gently, her ethereal

presence emanating warmth and comfort. "I'm here to help you."

"Am I... am I dying?" Maddie stammered, fear creeping into her voice.

"No, not yet," Makenna reassured her, placing a transparent hand on Maddie's shoulder. "But you need to keep fighting if you want to live."

"Tristen... he's trapped too," Maddie whispered, glancing at the wall of rubble that separated them.

"Then fight for him, Mads. Fight for yourself. You still have so much life left to live," Makenna urged, her eyes shining with love and determination. "Remember the strength we shared? It's still inside you."

Maddie felt a surge of energy course through her body, fueled by her sister's unwavering belief and the vivid memories they had shared. With newfound resolve, she turned her gaze to the pile of rocks, determination etched on her face.

"Okay, Kenna. For both of us," she said, her voice steady despite the pain in her battered hands.

"Good," Makenna nodded, her smile encouraging. "Now, start digging."

Maddie didn't hesitate. She reached for the nearest rock, wincing as its jagged edges bit into her skin. The weight of it was heavy, but she pushed through the discomfort, buoyed by her sister's spirit and the love they'd always shared.

"Keep going, Mads," Makenna urged, her voice filled with pride. "You're doing great."

As Maddie continued to dig, her hands scraped and bruised but determined, she felt a renewed sense of purpose. She would survive this ordeal for both herself and Tristen and for the love of the sister who'd never truly left her side.

"Thank you, Kenna," Maddie whispered, pausing for a moment to catch her breath. "I couldn't do this without you."

"Always, Mads," Makenna replied, her spirit beginning to fade as Maddie grew stronger. "I'll always be right here with you."

And with that, Maddie returned her focus to the task at hand, each rock she moved bringing her one step closer to freedom and to honoring the strength and love her sister had instilled within her. Sweat dripped down Maddie's brow as she strained to move another rock, her muscles burning with the effort. Her breaths came in shallow gasps, each inhale feeling like fire in her lungs. The pain was relentless, but she couldn't afford to stop now.

"Come on," Maddie muttered, gritting her teeth as she tried to wedge her fingers under a particularly stubborn stone. "You've got this, Maddie."

As she grappled with the debris that separated her from Tristen, she couldn't help but think of Makenna and how she had fought her own battle against leukemia. It gave her strength, knowing her sister's spirit was with her, urging her onward.

"Tristen?" Maddie called out, hoping for any sign that he was doing the same on the other side. A muffled response echoed back to her, spurring her on.

"Almost there, Mads," Tristen's voice sounded distant but determined. Where was he?

Maddie allowed herself a small smile at the sound of his words. Despite the fear and uncertainty that gripped her heart, she found solace in their shared determination to survive. She pictured him on the other side, mirroring her own efforts, and it filled her with a renewed sense of purpose.

"Okay," she whispered to herself, using every ounce of willpower she possessed to suppress the pain surging through her battered body. "Just a little more."

With each rock she moved, Maddie felt the weight of exhaustion pressing down on her. But she refused to let it claim her. Not when she knew that Tristen was fighting just as hard, that her father would be devastated if he lost both of his daughters and that Makenna's spirit was there beside her, cheering her on.

"Can't...give up..." Maddie panted, her vision starting to blur from the sheer exertion. She felt the sharp edges of a rock cut into her palm, but she barely registered the pain. All that mattered was getting through this obstacle and reuniting with Tristen.

"Almost there," she repeated Tristen's words like a mantra, drawing strength from their shared determination. "Almost there."

And as she continued to dig, every muscle in her body screaming in protest, Maddie clung to the love and hope that drove her forward — the memory of Makenna's courageous battle, the steadfast support of her father, and the unyielding bond she shared with Tristen.

"Almost there," she whispered once more, her voice barely audible beneath the sound of her labored breathing. But she knew, deep down, that they would make it through this together — just as they always had.

~*~

On the other side of the rock, Tristen's fingers trembled as he tapped out a desperate plea on his phone screen, careful not to let the sweat from his brow smudge the letters. "Dad... we need help. Maddie and I are trapped in a cave at the nature preserve. Hurry!"

He pressed send and held his breath, praying for a signal strong enough to transmit his message. The seconds dragged on like an eternity before, finally, his phone vibrated with a response.

"Stay where you are. We're coming."

Relief washed over Tristen, but it was short-lived as the reality of their situation set back in. They were still trapped, and Maddie was still separated from him by a wall of unforgiving rock.

"Please be okay, Maddie," he whispered, choking back a sob. He resumed digging, his hands raw and bloodied from the effort. Each stone he removed felt like a tiny victory, bringing him one step closer to the girl he loved.

~*~

Meanwhile, Daniel Grant raced through the streets, his heart pounding in his chest. He knocked on Robert Tyler's door with urgency, knowing that every second counted.

"Robert!" Daniel called out as soon as the door swung open. "Maddie and Tristen are trapped in a cave at the nature preserve. We need to go now!"

The color drained from Robert's face, but he didn't hesitate. Grabbing a flashlight and a rope, he joined Daniel in his car, and they sped off towards the preserve.

As they drove, the two fathers — who rarely saw eye to eye — found common ground in their shared concern for their children. Their past grievances seemed insignificant in the face of such danger.

"Tristen's never been one to give up easily," Daniel said, trying to reassure himself as much as Robert. "And Maddie...she's got her sister's spirit guiding her. They'll make it through this."

Robert's grip on the flashlight tightened as he thought about Makenna and the toll her fight against cancer had taken on their family. "Maddie's stronger than she thinks," he agreed, his voice thick with emotion. "She'll find a way."

The nature preserve loomed ahead, and the two men exchanged a look of grim determination. They would move heaven and earth to save their children, no matter what it took.

"Let's do this," Robert said, stepping out of the car. And together, they plunged into the darkness of the woods, guided by the unwavering light of a father's love.

The two hiked through the preserve without a sound. They were two fathers determined to make sure their children came out of this alive. The fire and rescue crew were on their way to help as well. While they would have been asked to stand aside, neither man had ever made it a plan to be on the sideline of anything in their lives before. They wouldn't start now.

The cave entrance yawned before them like the mouth of some ancient, slumbering beast. Within its depths, Tristen and Maddie were trapped, and Robert understood that every second counted. His heartbeat synchronized with the pounding of his feet on the damp earth as he and Daniel raced towards their children.

"Tristen!" Daniel called out, his voice echoing through the cavern as they entered. There was a moment of silence, and then a faint reply reached their ears.

"Da—Dad?"

"Son, we're coming! Just hold on!" Daniel shouted back, choking back tears. He and Robert exchanged a look of relief, knowing they had found him in time.

As they navigated the narrow passages, Robert felt the weight of his daughter's absence like a physical ache in his chest. The recent loss of Makenna had left a void in their family that seemed to grow larger by the day, and now Maddie was in danger, too. He couldn't — wouldn't — let her go.

"Tristen, where's Maddie?" Robert asked urgently once they reached the boy, who was bruised and covered in dust but otherwise unharmed.

"Over there," Tristen pointed, his voice shaking. "We got separated when the rocks fell."

"Stay with your father," Robert instructed his resolve steeling him for what lay ahead. "I'll find Maddie."

"Be careful," Daniel warned, placing a hand on

Robert's shoulder. It was a small gesture, but it carried with it the unspoken understanding that they were in this together.

"Always," Robert replied with a tight smile before plunging deeper into the cave.

~*~

Meanwhile, Maddie fought through the pain and exhaustion, clawing at the debris that buried her. She could feel her sister's presence lingering beside her, urging her to keep going. Makenna's spirit acted as both a balm and a driving force, allowing Maddie to push beyond her limits.

"Almost...there..." Maddie gasped, her fingers finally breaking through the surface of the rubble. She cried out in a mix of pain and triumph as she dragged herself free.

"Hey!" Robert's voice rang through the darkness, his flashlight beam cutting through the shadows like a lifeline. "I'm here, Maddie!"

"Da—Dad?" she croaked, relief flooding her senses.

"Right here," he confirmed, rushing to her side and helping her up. Maddie clung to him, her body wracked with sobs born from both physical anguish and an overwhelming love for her family.

"Thank God..." she whispered into his shoulder, tears streaming down her face.

"Your sister was with you, wasn't she?" Robert asked gently, his own emotions threatening to overwhelm him.

Maddie nodded, wiping away her tears. "She gave me the strength I needed."

"Let's get you home," Robert said, wrapping an arm around her as they made their way back toward Daniel and Tristen. As they walked, step by careful step, Maddie knew that despite the darkness that had enveloped them, love and hope shone brighter than any cave could ever contain.

Pale moonlight filtered through the cave's entrance as Maddie and the others finally emerged from the darkness. The fresh, cool air of the night enveloped them like a comforting embrace, soothing their raw nerves and battle-weary bodies.

"Thank you," Maddie whispered to Tristen, her voice hoarse from crying and exertion. "You saved me."

Tristen shook his head, his face flushed with emotion. "No, Maddie, we saved each other."

They shared a vulnerable smile, their connection deepened by the harrowing experience they had just endured together. Robert, his eyes glistening with unshed tears, placed a protective hand on Maddie's shoulder.

"Let's all be grateful for this moment," he said, his voice cracking. "We've been given a second chance — let's not waste it."

Maddie nodded, her heart swelling with a newfound appreciation for life and the people who mattered most. As they stood there, united in relief and love, she couldn't help but think of Makenna and the guiding spirit she had become.

"Hey, sis," she thought, feeling a gentle breeze brush against her cheek like a tender caress. "I know you're still with us...watching over us. I promise I'll live my life to the fullest for both of us."

A sense of peace settled over Maddie as she leaned into her father's embrace, allowing herself to absorb the strength and solace he offered. She knew that the road ahead would be filled with challenges, but with the memory of Makenna's spirit and the unwavering support of her family, she felt ready to face whatever life had in store.

"Let's go home," she murmured, her voice filled with determination and hope.

As Maddie took her first steps away from the cave, she felt the cold, damp earth beneath her feet, a stark contrast to the oppressive heat and darkness that had threatened to consume her not too long ago. Her family moved along with her, their footsteps echoing in unison as if they were one entity bound together by love and resilience.

"Can you believe we made it out of there?" Maddie asked, her voice shaking slightly, still coming to terms with the ordeal they had just survived.

"Because we stuck together, honey," her father replied, his strong arm wrapped protectively around her shoulders. "We're a team, remember?"

Maddie nodded, the truth of her father's words sinking in. They had faced the unimaginable — being trapped within the suffocating confines of the cave, separated by debris, and unsure of the fate awaiting them. But even against those odds, they had found a way out, guided by an invisible force that refused to let go.

"Hey, Tristen," Maddie said, glancing over at her friend, who was walking alongside her, his face pale but determined. "I'm really grateful for you, you know? You never gave up on me."

Tristen managed a weak smile, his eyes glistening with unshed tears. "The feeling is mutual, Maddie. I don't know what I would've done without you."

Lost in thought, Maddie considered the weight of the hardships they had faced together — the pain of losing Makenna to leukemia, the fear of being trapped in the cave, and the hopelessness that had nearly swallowed her whole. Now, however, she knew they could tackle anything life threw at them, no matter how daunting.

"Things will be different now," she mused aloud. "But we'll get through them together, right?"

"Absolutely," her father chimed in, her voice filled with love and reassurance. "We're stronger now, Maddie. And we'll face whatever challenges come our way as a family."

With every step they took away from the cave, the heavy burden of fear and despair seemed to lift, replaced by newfound hope. Maddie could feel it in the cool night air that brushed against her skin, in the gentle rustle of leaves overhead, and in the steady rhythm of her own heartbeat.

"Let's go home," she whispered, feeling more alive than ever before. In that moment, she knew that nothing could hold her back — not grief, not fear, and certainly not the darkness that had once threatened to consume her.

As Maddie walked arm-in-arm with her father, she felt the warmth of Makenna's spirit beside her, a guiding light that would never fade. Together, they would face the world, ready for whatever challenges that lay ahead.

Chapter 27

The sun cast a warm, golden hue on the spacious living room, its light glinting off the glass picture frames that lined the walls. Each frame held a memory of happier times before sorrow and loss had taken root in the hearts of Maddie Tyler and her family. The air was thick with emotion, laden with grief from the recent passing of Makenna, Maddie's twin sister.

Maddie sat on the plush sofa, her hands clasped together as she stared at the patterned rug beneath her feet. Her mind drifted to Tristen, the one person who had brought her comfort and solace amidst the storm of emotions that had engulfed her life. She could feel his warmth, his unwavering support, and most importantly, his love. She hadn't seen him since the cave-in. That was five days ago, and she already missed him.

"Sweetheart," Robert Tyler, Maddie's father, called out gently as he entered the room, pulling Maddie from her thoughts. His eyes were weary, dark circles beneath them revealing the emotional toll of losing a child. "Your mother and I need to talk to you about something."

"Is everything okay, Dad?" Maddie asked, concern etching her voice as she looked up at her father.

"Everything is fine," he assured her, taking a seat next to Maddie on the sofa. Jamie, Maddie's mother, soon followed, sitting down on her other side. They both looked at their daughter, love and concern filling their gaze. "We just want to talk about your relationship with Tristen."

"Here we go. Tristen has been really wonderful to me," Maddie said defensively, her heart racing at the thought of her parents disapproving of the one person who had helped her through the darkest days of her life.

"We know, honey," Jamie chimed in, placing a comforting hand on Maddie's arm. "We've seen how much he cares for you, and we're grateful for that. But there's some history between our families that you need to know about."

"History?" Maddie asked, her brow furrowing in confusion. Didn't she already know all there was to tell? Or were they just rehashing the same old thing all over again? "Your football rivalry again?"

"It was so much more than just a rivalry," her father tried to explain.

"Oh, I know all about your eye for an eye. You both were wrong, you know. Him for giving you a hard time and not having your back on the team, and you for getting him tossed out of the championship game. He lost his scholarship, you know," Maddie pointed out.

"He landed on his feet," grumbled Robert.

"So did you. You both need to let it go." Maddie crossed her arms over her chest and gave her dad a stern look.

"It's not always that easy," her father started to argue.

"Does this mean you don't want me to see him anymore?" Maddie whispered, tears welling up in her eyes as she sought reassurance from her parents.

"No, sweetheart," Jamie said softly, stroking Maddie's arm. "We just wanted you to understand why we might be... hesitant about your relationship with him."

"What?" Maddie couldn't believe the words that were coming out of their mouths. "But you said..."

"I know what I said, Maddie. Your happiness is what's most important to us," Robert added, his voice firm but filled with love. "But it won't be easy for our families to move past the conflicts we've had."

Maddie nodded, taking in her parents' words and understanding the complexity of the situation. She knew that it would take time for both families to heal, not only from the recent tragedy but also from the grievances of the past. But deep in her heart, she held onto the hope that her love for Tristen could help bridge the gap between their families and bring about healing for them all.

"Well, there's only one thing to do," her mother said.

"What's that?" Robert eyed his wife speculatively.

"Have dinner. Why don't you invite the Grants, Maddie?" Jamie suggested.

"Will do." Maddie was quick to get on it. She quickly texted Tristen and got his help with the request. Maddie was half afraid that they would refuse, but after a few minutes, Tristen texted her that he had managed to guilt them into it.

"Looks like we have a plan." Maddie smiled at her parents and felt the weight of a thousand bricks lift from her shoulders.

Maddie spent the rest of the afternoon in her room, trying to not let nervous energy overtake her. She opened a few of her books and got started on taking notes for class to catch up on some of the homework she had missed when she was out for a few days recovering from her injuries. When she had left the cave, she was bruised up pretty good, and her hands had been pretty scratched up, but at least she had been able to walk out. Maddie didn't care that there might still be treasure inside the caverns. She never planned to step inside them again.

When it was closer to dinner, Maddie kept an eye out for the Grants. When she saw them pull into the drive, she headed out to greet them. "Mr. Grant, Mrs. Grant."

"Mom, Dad, this is Maddie," Tristen introduced them.

Maddie stepped closer and reached for Tristen's hand as the sun dipped below the horizon. The warm glow of the setting sun seemed to cast a hopeful light on the situation, and Maddie couldn't help but smile at the thought.

"Are you sure you're ready for this?" Tristen asked, giving her hand a gentle squeeze.

"Ready as I'll ever be," she replied, steeling herself for the evening ahead. Tonight, their families would come together in an attempt to bridge the gap that lay between them, and Maddie knew that her love for Tristen was the key to paving the way for healing. "Please come inside."

As they stepped into the living room, Maddie noticed how both sets of parents seemed tense yet determined. Their eyes met briefly, acknowledging the weight of the moment that lay before them.

"Mom, this is Tristen," Maddie said, introducing him to her parents. She could feel his nervousness, like a current running between them.

"Hello, Mrs. Tyler. Coach," Tristen said politely, extending his hand to Robert and Jamie.

"Please, call me Jamie," Jamie replied, shaking his hand with a warm smile. "We've heard so much about you."

"And Robert, when we're not on the field," Robert added, clapping him on the back. "And these are my parents, Daniel and Susan Grant," he continued, gesturing towards Tristen's own parents, who stood nearby.

"Robert, good to see you. And nice to finally meet you, Jamie," Daniel said, stepping forward to shake hands with the Tylers.

"Likewise," Robert replied, nodding.

Over dinner, the conversation flowed more easily than any of them had anticipated. They spoke of memories and shared experiences, slowly building connections between them. But it was when Maddie and Tristen began to speak about their love for one another that a sense of profound understanding blossomed in the room.

"Ever since we met, Tristen has been my rock," Maddie said, her voice cracking with emotion. "He's supported me through the darkest times, and he understands what I've been through like no one else can."

"Likewise, Maddie has made me see the world and myself in a new light," Tristen added, looking tenderly at her. "We've grown together, and I can't imagine my life without her."

The parents exchanged glances, all of them touched by the depth of their children's love. Robert cleared his throat before speaking, his voice filled with emotion. "You know, Jamie and I have always wanted what's best for Maddie, and it's clear to us now that being with Tristen is a part of that."

"Daniel and I feel the same way," Susan chimed in, her eyes glistening with tears. "Seeing how much you two care for one another, despite everything that has happened in our families, is truly inspiring."

As the evening progressed, it became evident that Maddie and Tristen's love was a powerful force capable of bridging the gap between their families. Their ability to communicate and empathize with each other's families laid the groundwork for healing, and as they sat together in the flickering candlelight, hope began to take root in the hearts of everyone present.

"Tristen," Jamie began, her voice soft but firm, "Maddie has been through so much in such a short time, and we've seen how much she's grown since meeting you. You've helped her heal in ways we never thought possible."

"Thank you, Mrs. Tyler," Tristen replied quietly, his eyes locked with hers, reflecting the gravity of the moment.

Maddie could feel her heart pounding in her chest, waiting for what would come next.

Daniel stepped forward, placing a reassuring hand on his wife's shoulder. "We know our families haven't always seen eye to eye, but we can't deny the bond between you two. It's clear you both care deeply for each other, and we believe you're capable of nurturing and supporting one another."

"Seeing you two together," Robert added, his voice thick with emotion, "has shown us that love can overcome past grievances and misunderstandings. We'd be foolish to stand in the way of something so special." He paused for a moment, allowing the weight of his words to sink in before continuing. "Maddie, Tristen, you have our blessing to be together."

Maddie's breath caught in her throat, tears pricking at the corners of her eyes. She felt Tristen's hand squeeze hers gently, his own relief and joy radiating through the simple gesture. They glanced at one another, sharing a smile that conveyed more than words ever could.

"Thank you, Dad," Maddie whispered, her voice wavering with emotion. "And thank you to all of you. Your support means everything to us."

As the sun continued to set, casting its warm light over the gathering, Maddie and Tristen reveled in the relief and joy that washed over them. Their parents' blessing felt like a balm to their weary souls, mending the frayed threads that had once threatened to unravel their love.

With their families now united, the young couple realized they could face any challenge life might throw their way. Gratitude welled up within them, mingling with newfound hope for the future. In each other's embrace, they found solace, strength, and the promise of a love that would endure even the darkest of times.

Just a week later, their resolution was still going strong

as the families were now united for a common cause. The soft glow of twinkling fairy lights illuminated the faces of Maddie, Tristen, and their families as they gathered under a canopy of stars for the leukemia fundraiser. The event, held in the local park, was a bittersweet reminder of Makenna's battle, but it also served as a catalyst for healing.

"Remember, every dollar raised today will help someone like my sister," Maddie said, her voice steady and strong as she addressed the crowd. Robert and Jamie Tyler stood proudly beside their daughter, their eyes glistening with unshed tears.

As the evening progressed, it became evident that both families were making conscious efforts to work towards healing old wounds and rebuilding their relationships. Daniel and Susan Grant, Tristen's parents, engaged in heartfelt conversations with Robert and Jamie, actively listening and opening up about their own experiences.

"Robert, I must admit, I didn't fully understand the depth of the struggle your family has been going through," Daniel confessed, his gaze sincere. "But now, I see how important it is for us to support each other."

"It hasn't been easy," Robert admitted, nodding at Daniel's words. "But Maddie and Tristen have shown us that love can overcome even the deepest pain."

During the event, family members and friends took turns sharing stories about Makenna and discussing the impact of leukemia on their lives. They listened attentively to one another, validating each other's feelings and offering comfort.

Throughout the evening, Maddie and Tristen marveled at the progress their families were making. As they stood side by side, serving food and accepting donations for the cause, they couldn't help but feel an overwhelming sense of hope.

"Can you believe how far our families have come?"

Maddie whispered, her eyes shining with gratitude.

Tristen wrapped his arm around her shoulders, pulling her close. "It's incredible," he agreed. "And it's all because of you, Maddie. You've brought us all together."

Maddie shook her head modestly. "No, it's because of us, Tristen. Our love has done this."

As the night drew to a close, both families gathered together under the stars, pledging their commitment to continue working on their relationships and supporting one another through life's challenges. It was clear that the first steps towards healing had been taken, and the path ahead, though still uncertain, was illuminated by the light of newfound understanding and boundless love. Maddie glanced up at the stars one last time and found the hole that was always missing was now filled with so much light and hope that the future was wide open.

As a visionary storyteller and animal activist, Erik Daniel Shein blends his talent for children's and young adult writing with a passion for CGI animation and animal health and well-being. He has authored and co-written more than 30 novels and feature films, including the animated fantasy adventure tale, *The Legend of The Secret Pass* (Lions Gate Entertainment, 2019), which first began as a co-written novel by Erik and fellow author Melissa Davis. In addition to his writing, Erik is the founder and CEO of Shein Partnership LLC, a revered leader in the entertainment and publishing domains, and a producer, voice actor, and trained herpetologist.

Born in Southern Illinois, Melissa Davis fell in love with reading from an early age, so much so that she started writing when she was in the second grade. From poetry to short stories, she has a love for it all. When she was in high school, she attended the Illinois Summer School for the Arts at Illinois State University, which led her to attend the university. After graduating with a Bachelors in Education, Melissa taught for several years until her children were born, allowing her to fulfill two dreams at once: motherhood and penning her first books.

Since the age of twelve, Karen Fuller has loved the written word. She writes in a variety of genres, from Paranormal Romance to Young Adult and Middle-Grade. Recently, she has expanded her writing to screenplays as a team with Melissa Davis and Erik Shein. The writing team has several projects in the works. The future looks bright. Stay tuned for more to come.

www.ingramcontent.com/pod-product-compliance
Lightning Source LLC
Chambersburg PA
CBHW020729210626
46807CB00016B/543